If Only
Part 1

Frena Rhodes

ISBN: 979-8-35091-478-8

Dedication

I want to thank God for giving me the words and knowledge to write this story. I always say this book belongs to me and God.

I want to dedicate this book to my children Chris, David, and Sirr. They have been my cheering squad every step of the way since I began my writing.

Sometimes people's actions, including those we love and hold close to our hearts, can uproot our livelihood without us knowing, or even sometimes without them knowing, all the facts or the outcome of their actions or decisions.

I sit alone in my home, thinking about all the good and bad times my family has had here. My thoughts and my memories are troubled by problems that are rising, threatening my livelihood and the comfort of my home.

I stepped outside to the patio to look at all my husband and I had done together as far as planting and building our home. I wanted to be alone with my thoughts.

It is a beautiful day. The roses are beautiful, the grass pretty and green. This time of year, the grass is usually brown, I thought. I looked at each plant and flower that Colonel and I had planted together, remembering every detail that went into each plant's choice. He enjoyed working outside, and I enjoyed working right alongside him, humming, planting, and digging in the garden. Most of all, I enjoyed being his wife and friend. Most people find it hard to consider their spouse their best friend, but we could talk about anything. I sit here, thinking about the life I had with my husband Thomas, the Colonel, before he went home to be with God two years ago. I sit and think about the life I have with my children now. Colonel was such a gentleman; he served in the war and received numerous medals. Most of all, he was my hero. He was liked by everyone he encountered.

We were best friends before we were anything else.

Chapter 1

I DID NOT REALIZE THE TIME. THE ENJOYMENT OF MY OWN company sitting outside thinking about the past took all my attention until the ringing phone snapped me back to reality.

"Hello, Aunt Ophelia. How are you doing today?"

"I am doing well. How is my wonderful niece, and what time are you coming this morning?"

"Aunt Ophelia, you know this is Tuesday and I do not come on Tuesdays. What have you been up to?"

"Well, I know you don't work on Tuesdays, but I was feeling a bit left out today. I will find something to do to keep me busy."

"Okay, Auntie. I am going to stay home today and fix my husband a home-cooked meal. He has been working hard and late, so I am going to surprise him with his favorite meal today."

"Caroline, I am happy that you do that." Ophelia's voice softens, "I remember when I used to fix Colonel his favorite meals."

"I know you miss Uncle Colonel, Aunt Ophelia."

"I will talk with you later, Caroline. Have a good evening and tell that handsome nephew of mine I said hello."

"Okay, Aunt Ophelia. Have a good day.

I smile because I have the day all to myself and I can take this time to run all my errands. While I have the extra time, I am going to clean my biblical shrine. I take pride in my biblical shrine, which is a curio cabinet that holds my bible and the spiritual belongings I have collected over the years. I could feel the wrinkles in the corner of my mouth deepen as I began wiping down the shrine. Oh, there goes the phone again.

It was Sarah, Ophelia's best friend. They have been friends for over 20 years, and she has always been like a sister to Ophelia. She is always concerned about Ophelia's well-being, especially since she lost her husband, Colonel. "Hey precious, are you busy today?" asked Sarah.

"No, not yet," Ophelia replied.

Sarah asked Ophelia if she would like some company and that did not sound like a bad idea at all. She did not have to volunteer at the hospital today and Ophelia did not have any plans. They agreed to turn this day into a pampering day.

After getting off the phone with Sarah, Ophelia got herself ready; she was on her way to pick me up. *Sarah lives right down the block so she will be here in no time,* she thought. It was not difficult for her to find something to wear because all her clothes still look new; Ophelia rarely goes out. Thirty minutes later, she heard a knock at the door. Ophelia approached the door to open thinking, *good timing Sarah, you know me too well.*

"You didn't tell me you were going to be looking like a model, Sarah. You look nice, young lady," I greeted.

"Young lady?!" Sarah exclaimed. "Oh, how I wish! Girl, this is old. You know I do not get out much since I volunteer a lot at the hospital. Ophelia, why don't you come and volunteer at the hospital? They could use the help."

Ophelia had a feeling that Sarah would try to recruit her to become a volunteer, she loved to bring it up every chance she got. "I cannot do it Sarah; I would get too emotional there because I cannot handle watching people suffer with sickness." Sarah tried leaving it at that, but she still injected her last statement urging Ophelia to think about it. *I know Sarah better than anyone, she will ask again.*

"Okay, let's go enjoy ourselves," Ophelia said without holding back her enthusiasm.

As the day progressed, Sarah and Ophelia got pedicures, manicures, and went to a fancy restaurant to eat dinner. They both were excited to see their favorite show *"Columbo"* on the television at the nail salon.

"We should do this more often," Sarah exclaimed. "This day was much needed for the both of us." Sarah glimpsed over at me as she was driving me back home. "How are you doing Ophelia, really?"

"I am good, Sarah. I have my good days and bad days. When I talk with God, he always brings me through. I do get lonely and cry sometimes, but when I turn it over to God, I am alright. I always get up and move about doing other things to occupy my time. I love it when Caroline comes to clean for me. She doesn't have to, but she does."

Without hesitation Sarah asked, "Have you thought about dating, Ophelia?" Even though I was buckled down in the passenger seat, I felt like I was about to fall out of my seat when I heard her question.

"Girl, it is scary out there. I went on one date a few months ago. I met him at a grocery store. We got to talking and time passed. He asked if he could call me, and I told him yes. You know I have this extra phone number I give people when I am not sure how things are going to turn out. I gave him my number and sure enough, he called. It was unexpected. He was very polite. He asked if I wanted to go out to eat. I said sure. I told him I would meet him; I don't want anyone to know where I live. We met at this restaurant that he suggested. I didn't pray about the situation before going, I went on this date on my own. We went to a nice restaurant. He said to order what you want, so I did. I ordered filet and trimmings. We had a nice conversation. He started talking about his exes. I wasn't very interested; after the check came, he checked for his wallet and did not have it. I always go everywhere prepared. I told him I have the money for my meal, and I hope they work something out with you. I asked the waiter to bring me my ticket, I paid and said goodbye. I have not heard from him again. I am glad he had to stay, because I didn't want him trying to follow me home."

"My goodness, Ophelia, you should let someone know when you have a date. People are not very friendly anymore."

"I know, Sarah."

"You will find a nice person to be friends with. I know there is not another Colonel out there, but who God has for you is for you."

"Yes, I know."

"Remember to consider volunteering to keep your mind occupied. You would really enjoy it," Sarah urged.

There she goes, I knew she would ease this volunteering thing into the conversation again. "I will think about it. Thank you so much for today, Sarah, you are a wonderful friend."

Sarah dropped Ophelia off at her house and waited until she got inside safely before she drove off. *Well, I am tired now, but I am happy tired. I enjoyed my company and pampering. I enjoyed the meal and the conversations with a good friend. Oh goodness, gracious, as soon as I step into my house, the phone rings.*

"Hi, Ty'arra. How is my baby girl?"

"I am doing well, Mom."

"You missed Caroline today, didn't you?"

"Yes, I did. I called her and asked her what time she was coming this morning. She said you know I don't come today, Aunt Ophelia. I knew she didn't. At first, I did not have anything planned, but then Sarah called me with some wonderful plans for us."

"Good. How is she doing?"

"She is good, she invited me out today. We had a good time. We pampered ourselves with a manicure and pedicure."

"That was nice, Mom."

"Yes, it was, and we went out to eat. We had a good day. She was trying to talk me into volunteering at the hospital."

"That is a good idea, Mom. Why don't you do that?"

"I don't know, honey. The hospital makes me think about your father too much and I am a very emotional person."

"Mom, I know you miss Dad. But you need to move around a little, as the young people say."

Ophelia had to agree with her daughter's words of wisdom because she does need to move around more. Her conversations with her daughter have always been so insightful. She is so amazed at the bright young lady she has blossomed into. Ty'arra keeps her included in every aspect of her life. She mentioned to Ophelia that she is going to the beach with some of her college friends. "We are going to head out this Friday and we will be gone for the weekend. "Is that okay, Mom?" she asked, as if to still seek Ophelia's approval.

"Sure honey. You all enjoy yourselves. I hope this is not going to interfere with your studying."

"It won't. I am good. I love you, Mom."

"I love you too, sweetie. Be very careful. Bye-bye."

Let me check the mailbox, I hate to but need to. Oh goodness, another letter from the IRS. This is unbelievable! I opened the letter up and began reading:

Dear Mrs. Roberson, this is your second notice concerning the back taxes that are due. We need to hear from you as soon as possible. You need to send in $100,000 by check or money order.

> *What makes them think I have that kind of money? My daughter is in college and my sons have families. God, what do I do? I am already paying a second mortgage Colonel took out on the home without telling me. What do I do? Well, I am not going to worry about it because I have had a good day and the IRS is not going to spoil it.*

═══

I slept well last night. I guess it was from me and Sarah getting out yesterday. Good morning, God, and please tell my Colonel I said good morning. I better get dressed. I think Caroline just came in.

7

"Auntie, are you okay? You seem preoccupied."

"I am fine, dear. Did my nephew enjoy his special meal yesterday?"

"He did, Auntie; I need to do that a little more often. He is so sweet. He tells me I don't have to cook, but I enjoy cooking for him. What did you do yesterday?"

(Silence)

"Auntie, what did you do yesterday?"

"Honey, I am sorry."

"Are you sure there is nothing wrong?"

"I am good. You know my neighbor, Sarah. She called me and we went out yesterday and had a wonderful time. We pampered ourselves."

Caroline smiled with joy in her heart because she was happy her aunt had gone somewhere to enjoy life. The last time she had seen her aunt have fun was when Colonel was alive. Caroline asked if she needed her to do anything special in the house before she started her usual tasks. "No, you can just do the usual. Take your time," Ophelia replied. She headed toward the stairs heading to her room, "I will be attending church tonight, because I've missed quite a bit."

"Are you okay, Auntie?"

"Yes, I am fine. I will be back."

The phone rings.

"Auntie, you want me to get the phone?"

"Yes, dear. Tell whoever it is that I will call them back."

"Hi, Jarrett," Caroline says. "What's up?"

"Nothing's up. Caroline, is Mom there?" Jarret, Ophelia's oldest son, called to check in on his mother. Caroline's eyes fixated on the stairs Ophelia went up a few minutes ago,

"Yes, she is upstairs. Jarrett, she has been acting a little withdrawn this morning. I wonder if everything's okay."

Concern grew on Jarret's face, but he answered, "As far as I know it is. Could you have her pick up the phone please?"

The struggle was real to keep worry from settling in Ophelia's voice as she picked up the phone. "Hi, son. How are you doing?"

"I am fine, Mom, how are you? Caroline said you seem a little withdrawn this morning. Are you okay?"

"Yes, son, I am. How is the family?"

"Everyone is doing well. Would you tell me if something was wrong?"

The lie just slipped through my teeth, "Of course, I would." *There is no way I can have anyone else in the family take on the concern with this IRS mess.* I quickly changed the subject. "I talked with Ty'arra last night. She is going to the beach this weekend."

"That girl is so spoiled. You didn't spoil me and Jason the way you spoiled her."

"Sure, we did."

"What are your plans for the weekend since Ty'arra is not coming home?"

"Well, I haven't thought that far ahead yet."

"Well, you could fly out and see us and visit with the grandkids. They would love to see you."

Jarrett and I drifted from one topic to another. I told him that I would like to attend my church revival every day this week.

The sound of Caroline's voice made me realize that it was dinner time. "Auntie, are you coming down?"

"Yes, I will be down in a minute."

After Ophelia hung up with Jarrett on the phone, she began staring at Colonel's picture on the dresser beside her bed.

Colonel, I am in a financial mess, and I am so used to you taking charge. I have gotten myself into a bind and I don't even know how. I haven't taken out any loans and I didn't know we owed the government any money. I get my taxes done every year. I don't know what is going on. I should have paid these back taxes they are saying I owe before I went on those cruises and before I paid two years of Ty'arra's college tuition. But now I am faced with this situation. God, please help me. Tell me what to do.

Chapter 2

"AUNT OPHELIA, YOU WANT ME TO CLEAN YOUR GOSPEL shrine today? I don't think I cleaned it when I was here last."

"I cleaned it myself, Caroline. Thanks anyway."

"You want me to fix our lunch today? What do you feel like eating?"

"Something light. I don't feel like eating anything heavy this early. I have a lot to do before I leave."

"Okay, a light lunch it is," Caroline replied.

"So, Jarrett wants you to fly out there for the week?"

"Yes, how did you know?" I asked.

"You know I know how close these kids of yours are to you. That is great. I miss my mom, too. I thank God for you, Aunt Ophelia."

"Your mom and I were so close growing up and I know she has been gone now three years, but I miss her very much," Ophelia reminisces.

"That was my sister you are talking about. We were always close. Mother or Dad wouldn't have had it any other way. We would talk for hours at night. We had our faults, too. She always wanted to be like Dad and follow in his footsteps. I don't know why she wanted to be in the military. That was her passion. But she met your dad and just fell in love. He was a lot like your grandfather. He was very respectful. He was a loving person too, He changed drastically right before our eyes. the change wasn't good." Ophelia reminisced. "They had two beautiful children when they had you and Patrick. I don't know what is wrong with Patrick."

"I know, Auntie. He is going through a lot; he can't get a decent job, he doesn't have luck with girls, I could go on, but you get the picture."

"You know yourself that Patrick is not applying himself," Ophelia replied.

"He wants things handed to him; he is lazy and stuck on himself. So much for all that. I don't want to reminisce now or talk about Patrick. Your lunch is ready," Caroline said.

"This looks good, Caroline."

Caroline had fixed two sub sandwiches with lettuce, tomatoes, cucumbers, microgreens, pepper jack cheese, and hard salami. She had arranged both sandwiches on the plate. "It looks like the sandwiches I see on the food channel," Ophelia added.

"Thank you. I just put something together out of the refrigerator."

"Did you enjoy your lunch, Auntie?" Caroline asked later.

"Yes, I did. I am going to go outside into the garden for a few minutes. I just want to be outdoors for a while. It is supposed to get cold later in the evening."

"Are you sure you are okay, Auntie?"

"I told you, baby, I am okay," I replied.

"I am going to clean up here. I will clean the rooms upstairs after that, and then I am done for the day, unless you want me to do something else."

"No, go ahead. But come back before you leave."

Oh, my goodness! The joy of being in my garden just tantalizes my soul. It is like being in an outdoor sanctuary for me. I could stay out here all day and I would not complain, no matter how good or bad the weather is. I can hear the birds clearly on this beautiful day and I feel like they are relaying a message from the Lord to me in tune.

"Auntie, you have a phone call," Caroline called from the back door.

"Who is it?"

"It is Jason."

"Okay, thanks. I will be right in. I was enjoying being outside and listening to the birds sing."

"Hi, son, how are you doing?" Ophelia greeted her youngest child.

"The family and I are good. How are you, my special lady?"

"I am good, Jason."

"You wouldn't be just saying that to me, would you?"

"Son, no, I am good."

"Jarrett said he asked you to come out this weekend because Ty'arra is not coming home."

"Yes, he did, but I told him I would like to attend the revival we are having this week at the church. I will be seeing all of you in a few months. You know the holidays are coming up. This year is going so fast. How is Suzette?"

"She is good. Look who she has for a husband."

"Yes, I know," Ophelia replied, laughing lightly.

"Okay, Mama, I will check with you later and see if everything is okay. Please call me if you need to. Love you, Mom."

"I love you too, son."

"Tell Caroline I said 'bye,' and thank her for being there to help you."

Ophelia hung the phone up to head back outside as Caroline came down the stairs to catch up with her.

"Auntie, I am going to leave. I have cleaned the upstairs and downstairs. I want to get home before Andrew does."

"Okay, honey, I understand. Thanks so very much. I know you don't have to come and do this, but I really enjoy your company." We hugged and Ophelia kissed her on the cheek before she left.

Admiring God's beautiful earth is so breathtaking. God orchestrated the seasons so well, and the earth shows its beauty in each season. I can tell the fall is coming, and that is my favorite time of year.

"Hi Mrs. Ophelia," a voice came over the fence. "I hope I didn't startle you; you seem like you are in deep thought." I turned around and saw that it was my neighbor across the street, named Tim.

"Hello neighbor, and no, you didn't. I am doing well. How are you doing in school?"

"School is okay, Mrs. Ophelia. I am going to feed my dogs. Please call me if you need help with anything."

"I will, Tim. Thanks."

I thank God for all my neighbors. Everyone is friendly. Sometimes we get a little loud music coming through here, but they keep going. It is still wise to be careful, though, because people never know what can happen. I guess it is time for me to go in and get myself together for church tomorrow.

Chapter 3

CAROLINE WALKS INTO HER HOUSE.

"Hi, honey. You are home. How was your day?" she asked her husband, Andrew.

"It was a good day. How was your day with Aunt Ophelia?"

"It was a good day too, but I think something is bothering her. She won't say anything, though."

"You think it is something serious?" Andrew asked.

"Yes, I think it is," she replied.

"Wait until she brings it up to you Caroline. "Don't pry," he advised.

"I won't, baby," she said.

"Something strange happened at the office today," Andrew continued. "I was in my office and my secretary called and said I had a client. I asked her to have them take a seat, as I would be out in a few minutes. When I went out, I just happened to glance up and saw a man walking by. I could only see the back of him, but I thought it was Patrick. My secretary said that is the guy who wanted to see me, he just got up and left. Have you talked with Patrick lately?"

"No, I haven't spoken with him. I hope he is all right. Aunt Ophelia and I were talking about him today. He needs to get control of his life and do something with it," Caroline said.

"Caroline, let's not jump to any conclusions. I am not sure it was him. Call him when you get a chance, though. Maybe he'll say something about it," Andrew said.

"Okay, I will."

"What's for dinner? I am starved," her husband asked.

"We are having one of your favorite meals. Lamb chops, mixed vegetables, and mashed potatoes."

"That sounds delicious. I will wash up and we can eat."

———

Thank God, I made it to church because I have really missed the fellowship.

"Hello Sister Ophelia. How are you doing tonight?" the greeter asked.

"Just fine, Brother Michael, and yourself?" I responded.

"I am doing wonderfully, I won't complain.

The choir is singing my favorite song, Hold on to God's unchanging hands. I get lost in God when I hear that song. God, please help me with my financial situation. As I listen, I am still praying and asking God for help. Thoughts circulate through my mind as I sat there in church, caught up in my own world and begging God to intervene.

When the minister gave his topic for the night, I wondered if he was talking to me or did, he know my situation? Maybe it is what I needed to hear. The topic was God may not come when you want him, but He is always on time.

He said, "God's time is not our time. That doesn't mean stop trusting and stop giving your situation to Him."

It is so easy for us to give up.

He said, "You can be on our knees praying, and you get a knock at the door. It is the mailman. You must sign a certified letter. You start shaking, wondering 'What is this?' It is a letter saying that you either pay this bill

IF ONLY: PART I

in a few days or your property or car or whatever will be repossessed. You
get scared and throw your hands up, and then say 'If it isn't one thing, it is
another.' If you live on this side, you are going to have bills and unpaid bills.
Trust in God. If you can see ways to resolve these issues, go ahead and do so."

"God is so good, and we cut him short all the time," the minister continued.

*As the minister was talking, I was praying and asking God for help. Maybe
He did give me help before I went on my trips, but that can't be.*

I enjoyed the singing, the praying, and the message tonight.

*I better head home since it is getting late. I did not wear a jacket and it is
cold out tonight.*

Chapter 4

TY'ARRA AND HER FRIENDS WERE PACKING FOR THEIR upcoming trip. Stephanie got a few of her clothes and placed them in her suitcase. She looked over at Ty'arra and saw the look of concentration on her face as she packed everything she could fit into her suitcase.

"Ty'arra, what are you doing?" Stephanie asked.

"Stephanie, you know me. I want to be prepared for anything," Ty'arra replied.

"We are all ready and packed. Are you taking everything you have?" Stephanie rolled her eyes and continued, "We are only going for two days."

"I must be prepared, Stephanie," Ty'arra insisted. "I am ready, okay? We can go get in the car."

"Hi Roger and Craig," Ty'arra greeted her friends.

"Good thing you have a van, Craig," Stephanie announced, "because Ty'arra packed all her clothes!"

Everyone laughed at Ty'arra, but she didn't care. She had what she needed. They were taking the two-hour road trip to South Carolina. They were beach bound and anything could happen.

"I had to bring homework," Ty'arra said. "I have an exam on Monday. I can work while we're driving."

"Girl, this is supposed to be a fun trip," Roger said.

"I can't neglect my responsibilities." Ty'arra said. "My mother would hang me alive. You worry about yourself, Roger." Ty'arra turned toward Stephanie, "You have an exam on Monday, too."

"I know. I will study when I get back," Stephanie replied.

"Well, I don't want to take a chance. We don't know what could happen," Ty'arra said.

"Hey, Ty'arra, Stephanie. You want a hit?" Roger asked.

"Do I want a hit of what, Roger?" Ty'arra responded.

"This relaxer. It will help you study, Ty'arra."

"I don't need anything to help me study, Roger," she replied.

"I'll take one, Roger," Stephanie interrupted.

"That doesn't smell too good. Will you put down a window, please? I know students try different things while they are in college, but smoking weed, and cigarettes are not my thing. I am not judging you all, to each his own, but I don't want any," Ty'arra said.

"We understand, Ty'arra. I hope I didn't offend you," Roger said.

"You didn't offend me. I hope we don't get stopped by the police for anything, though," Ty'arra replied.

"We are okay. This doesn't get you high, it relaxes you," Craig said.

"Don't get too relaxed … you are driving."

"Craig, did you understand the professor when he asked everyone to write an essay?" Ty'arra asked.

"Yes," he replied.

"Do you remember what the essay is supposed to cover and what topics he gave us to write on?"

"I left those notes in the dorm," he replied. "He gave us three. I know one he asks how you would handle a situation if you saw a doctor do something to a patient that you knew wasn't right and he looked up and saw you watching him. The other one is what you would do if a patient asked you to do something that you knew wasn't right. I can't remember what the third question was, though."

"Okay. Thank you, Craig, that helps," Ty'arra replied.

Roger rolled his eyes, "Girl, you are taking this college stuff all too serious,"

"I am just trying to pass my classes," Ty'arra replied. "My mother paid too much hard-earned money for me to go to school, and I want to do my best. She is not a doctor like your father or a counselor like your mom. Even if she was, I want to make my own money. When I leave college, I want the grades to go with me. You need to think about what you are doing, too, Roger. You want to live off your parents for the rest of your life?"

"I have my own dream, Ty'arra," Roger replied.

"I want to have my own home and everything," Ty'arra said. "I appreciate what my parents have sacrificed for me to be able to go to college."

"Excuse me, everyone," she added. "I am going to call my mom and let her know we are on our way to the beach."

"Hey, Mom," Ty'arra said. "I called to tell you we are on our way. Should be there within the next thirty minutes. Are you okay?"

"Yes, honey. I just got in from church, and I enjoyed it so much," Ophelia replied.

"I am happy for you."

"You all please stay alert and please be careful on the road," Ophelia said. "Call me when you get settled in?"

"Ok, Mom, I will," Ty'arra replied. "Mom, don't forget to go put flowers on Dad's grave."

"I already did that."

"Thank you, Mom. I will talk with you later," Ty'arra said.

"I don't call my parents and let them know where I am going," said Roger.

"I do," Ty'arra said. "Because there is so much going on. At least if something happen my mother will know where I am."

"Ty'arra, that is a good thing calling your mother and letting her know where you are and who you are with," Craig said.

"Thank you, Craig."

Chapter 5

OPHELIA WAS SITTING ALONE ON HER BED AND A SMILE crept over her face. *Oh, Colonel, I miss you so much. Honey, I am so proud of our children, especially Ty'arra, our only daughter. I know you spoiled her rotten and I did too, but she knows what she wants out of life. Time for me to lay this body down. I love you, Colonel. God be with me and all my endeavors.*

Sleep drifted over her as she ended with her nighttime prayer.

Good morning, Father. This is the day God has made. Good morning, Colonel. I am not going to call Caroline this morning, I am going to let her rest and enjoy her husband. Today, I am going to do something different. Working outside yesterday was refreshing for me. Colonel and I used to work on our beautiful garden together, so that is where I will spend most of my day. I feel as if I am near him when I go to the garden. It is very peaceful out in the backyard. There are a lot of beautiful memories in the garden. That is my chore for the day.

Before I do anything, though, I am going to get this dreadful phone call over with. I have got to call the IRS. Where did I put my IRS folder?

"Your call is very important to us, please stay on the line. There are fourteen calls ahead of you."

I am not going to sit on this phone to talk with the IRS. I will call later.

Good morning to all my biblical ornaments. God is so good to me, and I know he is going to see me through whatever the situation may arise or already here.

Well, here I go outside in my Garden of Eden. I love it out here, but sometimes it is depressing because I miss Colonel. I hear birds singing, it is so peaceful.

Looking around at all my neighbor's houses, I know they are probably all gone to work or getting ready to go to work. Except for Sarah. She is probably having breakfast with her husband, if he is back in town.

This is the day that the Lord has made. I am going to rejoice regardless of the situation. I am not going to let Satan or Internal Revenue steal my joy. Here comes Sarah, never with a hair out of place, always beautiful and always matching.

"If I have never told you, Ophelia, it is a joy living in the same neighborhood as you!"

"When weeks pass without us seeing each other, I feel the same way. How is it going at the hospital?" Ophelia asked.

"Oh, Ophelia, I am enjoying every minute of it. I guess because I enjoy helping people any way I can. I am telling you; you would enjoy it too."

"I know, Sarah, but I am too emotional, especially since Colonel passed away in the hospital. I miss him so much," I said.

"I know you do."

"It will be two years this Thanksgiving, and I am already dreading the holidays."

"I can't tell you how to feel, Ophelia, but it might help you to get out more often. Come work with me," Sarah coaxed.

"Let me think about it a little while. I enjoy looking at all of the flowers and plants at this time of year. You know, Colonel and I did all this together."

"I know that is why you are out here. I have noticed when you are going through something very troubling, or any time you just want to be near him, you come out here," Sarah replied. "What is going on, Ophelia? We have been neighbors too long for you to hide something from me."

"Thanks for asking, Sarah, but it is something I have got to work out by myself. Nothing serious, just pressing. I will work it out. If I can't get it worked out, believe you me, I will come calling."

"No, you will not, but please don't hesitate to ask or call on me if you need someone to talk to," Sarah replied.

"Thanks, Sarah, I will. I apologize, where are my manners? Would you like a cup of coffee?"

"I would, thank you," Sarah replied.

"Let's go in, we can talk in there unless you would rather stay out here."

"Sarah, you remember when Colonel and I and you and John went to Colorado for the weekend?" Ophelia asked as she carried mugs and the coffee pot to the kitchen table.

"I do remember. We had such a wonderful time. I was just thinking about that last week," Sarah replied. "We are not just neighbors. I think in another life we were probably related."

"I feel the same way. Anyway, on that trip it seemed like we had only ourselves and we were content."

"I know. Ophelia, are you okay?" Sarah asked.

"Yes, just missing my other half. He seemed to make everything alright."

"I would stick around so we could talk more. I am off today, but there is a patient I want to check on. I know something is on your mind that is troubling you, but I have got to go and get ready to go to the hospital. Are you sure you are going to be alright?"

"Yes, Sarah I am going to be alright."

I guess I should have asked Sarah about a part-time job at the hospital. But then I would have to go into detail because I need to work. I don't think I am ready to open my business like that, especially without knowing the details of what the business is all about.

Chapter 6

WELL, I AM AT THE HOSPITAL. IT IS VERY COLD OUT HERE. IT wasn't this cold when I was talking to Ophelia outside, Sarah thought.

"Good morning, Sarah. I thought you were off today."

"I am, but I decided to come in to check on Mr. Robertson. How is he doing today? I have taken a liking to him because he reminds me so much of a friend's late husband," Sarah said.

"That is nice of you, Sarah. He will be happy to see you."

"Good morning, Mr. Robertson," Sarah greeted her favorite patient.

"Good morning to you, Sarah. What are you doing here today? I asked about you, but I was told you were off."

"I am off, but you are such a good patient I wanted to come in today and check on you," Sarah replied.

"Thank you so very much."

"Have your son or church members been out to see you this morning?" Sarah asked.

"No, only you, and you are such a pleasure to see," Mr. Robertson replied, a twinkle in his eye.

"Oh, thank you Mr. Robertson."

"I wish you would call me Robert."

"Okay, I will."

"May I ask you something?"

"Yes, sure Robert," Sarah replied.

"What makes me so special?"

"Well, I enjoy talking to you because you are pleasant regardless of your situation. There's nothing too hard for God. I know, Robert, there is something special about you. You remind me so much of a friend's late husband. He was a wonderful man."

"I do?"

"Yes, you do," Sarah said. "I enjoy you as a person and a child of God. Let us leave it as that, okay?"

"Sure, that is fine with me," Robert said.

———

When Ty'arra made it to the beach with her friends, she immediately called her mom to let her know they had arrived safely. Ty'arra realized as she relaxed on the beach how much she needed a break from studying and working non-stop.

"Mom, I needed this break. I miss being with you, but I am enjoying myself."

"Okay, be careful and watchful. Don't hesitate to call if you need me. Love you, sweetie," Ophelia said.

"Love you too, Mom."

"Okay, Ty'arra, you have gotten your mama call over with. Let's go and have some fun. The beach is calling us," said Stephanie. "The beach is calling us!"

"Okay, Stephanie, I am ready."

"I might find me a rich husband out here," Stephanie said, laughing.

"Stephanie, you don't need that right now. Don't you have enough problems?"

"Ty'arra, I enjoy life to the fullest."

"Stephanie, you are not doing too well in school, and you are not even concerned. Don't you feel bad, wasting your parent's money the way you are doing?"

"Don't try to lay any guilt trip on me now, Ty'arra, because I am here to have fun. I will worry about grades and all that when I get back. No serious talk, Ty'arra, it is playing time," Stephanie insisted.

"Let's let the boys be boys. They may not want us to follow them. You know boys," Ty'arra said.

"Yes, I do," Stephanie agreed with a grin.

"I just want to lie in the sun for a while and then get in the water. It is going to get cool later."

"You know we don't do too well in the sun," Stephanie cautioned her friend.

"Yeah, right. This is life."

"Ty'arra, I am going to the water. See you in a few," Stephanie said.

Later, Ty'arra saw Stephanie with several figures, standing near the water.

Well, I guess Stephanie found her rich man. They are all close, but it seems like she is upset. I guess I need to go out and see what is wrong . . .

"Stephanie, are you okay?" Ty'arra asked her friend.

"Yes, I am fine. Relax."

I continue to observe Stephanie and her friend. It seems as if they know one another.

I am not comfortable. Things are getting kind of hostile between those two. "Stephanie, are you okay?" Ty'arra repeated.

"If you don't leave me alone, I will call the police," said Stephanie, angrily.

"You call the police, and I will tell them you and your mother are murderers," the man said angrily.

"Leave me alone, Leonard," Stephanie said, turning away.

"I am sorry, Ty'arra. Of all places I had to run into the devil," she added.

"What is it?" Ty'arra asked.

"I have a past that I am not proud of, and I had to come on vacation and find a part of it. I don't feel like swimming."

"What is it?" Ty'arra repeated quietly.

"You want to go back to the room? I don't feel comfortable." Stephanie said, ignoring Ty'arra's question.

"Sure, let me get my things."

"Ty'arra, I don't go around telling everyone my business, but I am going to tell you a small portion of my past because if anything happens while I am here someone else will need to know what to do. The gentleman, the devil, I was talking to at the beach, well, he raped me when I was fifteen years old," Stephanie said as they hurried back to their hotel room. "I was a little disobedient; my parents didn't want me to have a boyfriend at that age. I was very defiant. He is the son of one of my father's colleagues, and he is a lot older than I am. I thought he was so cute and loving ..."

"He would always look at me and smile," Stephanie continued. "I didn't want to do anything with him, I just wanted him to be nice to me and we just kissed. I know it was wrong, but my parents were too busy for me. My mom had her job and friends, and my dad was very busy with his job and friends. I had all the material things I wanted, but I didn't have my parents. Leonard felt like a father, and a friend who cared. One night my parents were not home. The babysitter was there. I called and asked Leonard to come over. So, I put some of my mom's sleeping pills in the babysitter's drink so she would not know anything. I told him what I did, and he was happy. I was only fifteen at the time and he was twenty-nine, you would think he would know better. Anyway, he came over to my house. I just wanted him to hold me and kiss me, and after that he said he wanted to play a game. He got up to check on the housekeeper, she was fast asleep in the den, knocked out. He came back in and turned the lights down. I said, "What are you doing?" He said he was making it cozy so we can play a game. I said, "Okay, what game are we going to play?" He said, "Mom and Dad." I told him I didn't want to play that game. He said he was the oldest, so after we played his game then we would play my game."

"Okay, like I said I was only fifteen, but I thought I knew this man even though I had only seen him a few times. He knew I liked him, but he turned the lights down and he came toward me, and my smile began to lessen a little, because something did not feel right. He pulled me down on the sofa gently and began to kiss me. I liked that, but I did not like it when he started bothering my clothes. He said to hold on, he was going to be gentle with me. That's when I said, "I am a kid, don't do this. He said I was a mature kid, and he noticed how I watched him. He said he was not going to hurt me …"

Stephanie was crying softly as she continued, "I told him, 'Please don't do this.' I couldn't scream or do anything. He pulled my panties down and unzipped his pants. I was crying. He got upset with me and he said, 'You know you want this. I believe in giving kids what they want.' I screamed, and he slapped me and told me to shut up. When he was done, he told me not to tell my parents anything, but they would not believe me because I had already been in trouble, I was a troublemaker. I continued to cry. I ran to the bathroom and took a long hot shower, crying and crying. I tried to wash his smell and everything about him off me. I felt dirty and alone. When I went back downstairs, he was gone. I knew my parents would be home soon. The babysitter would be coming around in a few, because I didn't give her very much. My parents came home. I was still upset, and I started crying. They asked me what was wrong, and I began to tell my parents what happened. I thought the first thing they would do was call the police and take me to the hospital …"

"I told them everything I did, including putting a sleeping pill in the babysitter's drink. I planned the whole thing, I thought. But I didn't plan on him raping me. My parents asked me to leave the room. Before I left the room, the babysitter came out of the den and apologized to my parents for falling asleep. She was upset; she said this had never happened before. She said I hope everything is alright. I am very sorry. I was hoping they would not tell the babysitter everything, and they didn't. They assured her it wasn't her fault. They told her she could leave. She left and I went upstairs. Ty'arra, I am telling you this in secrecy. I haven't told this to anyone but you. I hate to ask you this, but please don't tell Craig or Roger. This is embarrassing to me and my family."

"Stephanie, I will not tell your business," Ty'arra said.

"I hope nothing happens, but I am letting you know in case it does. Do you remember what he looked like, Ty'arra?"

"Yes, I do."

"Let me finish the story of that long night," Stephanie said. "After going upstairs, I could hear my parents talking. My dad didn't want any publicity and my mother didn't either, so they called me downstairs. They told me it was my fault this happened. I said I know because I invited him over and I put a sleeping pill in the babysitter's drink. I understand that, but I didn't ask him to rape me. They told me that I did ask for it, when I went to all that trouble inviting him over. I was so hurt, Ty'arra. They said we will be talking to his parents, but we are not going to get the police involved. He lived with his parents. Then my mother said that tomorrow she would take me to the doctor and tell them I was with a boy without their permission, and they just wanted to make sure I was okay. They said they would take it from there. After that, I never saw Leonard again. I did go to the doctor the following day. The doctor said it was too early to tell if I was pregnant."

"Mom drove me back home in silence. After we got home, Mother told me to go to my room, as I was on punishment for two weeks. I tried to tell my mom that I didn't ask that man to rape me. She said that I probably didn't, but my body posture and the way I talked with him gave him the go-ahead, and by putting that sleeping pill in the babysitter's drink I basically asked for it. My mother looked at me with cold eyes and told me that I may not think my parents love me, but they do and what I did was very wrong. Mother said she didn't know how she felt. Then she said I was determined to disgrace this family when I had everything. Under my breath I said, 'Yes, everything but my parents.'"

"As the weeks went by, I did start noticing a change in my body and every morning I felt sick. I have had enough friends tell me how it felt when they were pregnant. I was so disappointed and hurt. I was pregnant, fifteen and pregnant. What was I going to do? I went to my mom, and I told her I thought I was pregnant. She asked me how I knew. I told her I was having morning sickness and my body was changing. She made an appointment for me to see the doctor again."

"It was confirmed," Stephanie continued. "The doctor said with me being so young and small I might not carry the baby full term. Mother thanked the doctor and we left. I cried, I said, 'Mama, what am I going to do? I am too young to be pregnant.' My mother told me I had to keep it to myself and not tell anyone, not a soul. When we got home, Dad was there. I went to my room. Mother told him, and they went to their room. Thank God it was summer. I didn't want to go to school and face anyone, because those girls seemed to be able to tell when someone was pregnant."

"Anyway, there was a week of silence in the house between my parents and me. They were talking to each other, but not to me. And then a month went by, and I had gone out for the day with a friend. I asked her to bring me home early, since I wasn't feeling too good. I went to my room, and I felt something wet in my panties. I went to the bathroom, and I was bleeding. It was early, so Mom was still at work. I called her and told her I was bleeding. She asked me if I did anything to myself. I said no, I have been out all day with a friend. She said she was coming home. Before she could get home, I started hurting badly. When she got there, I told her, 'I hurt really bad, Mom.' She took me to the hospital and told them my situation. Thank God no one was there that we knew. At least we thought there wasn't. The nurse took me to a room and checked and told me I was having a miscarriage."

"But at the hospital that night, Leonard was in the waiting area. We didn't know he was there. The doctor didn't keep me overnight, she just did what she had to do and sent me home. She told my mother what to expect and for me to stay in bed for a couple of days."

"On the way home, I don't know how I felt, but I felt like I left something or someone at the hospital and I couldn't go get it back. My mother told me, 'You see, God don't like ugly. That is why you lost the baby.' I was so upset with my mother. I told her, 'I have never heard you pray to God or even talk about God, but now you are bringing up His name.' I know I was disrespectful, but I told her, 'Please don't talk to me. You don't know how I feel, nor have you asked me how I feel.' I was hurting inside and mentally. My father was coming home when we got there. He asked me how I was feeling, and I told him I wasn't feeling too good. He gave me a hug and told me to go to bed. I felt as if I grew up overnight. That is my story, and it didn't come back to me to affect me until I saw him today."

"I don't know if I hate him, or just that his presence makes me feel uneasy. After all, I did invite him to my house. The reason I am telling you this is because he was out there calling me a murderer. He told me he was at the hospital when my mother and I came into the emergency room. I was holding my stomach, and he knew then that I was pregnant, and it was his child. He knew I was a virgin. He had moved out of his parent's house and had gotten his own place out of town, but he was at the hospital because a friend of his had gotten sick at his place and he took him to the hospital. Today he said, 'I heard your mother say, "Do what you must do to protect my daughter. Whatever it takes or whatever you must take." I knew then that she was saying 'take the baby.' He said he didn't know how to contact me. Then he said he knew he would see me again and then he would tell me that me and my mother are murderers. He said he was not going to say anything, but he might try to find a way to make that happen again or do something else instead. Be watchful."

Ty'arra reached out to give her best friend a hug.

"Stephanie, my mother always tells me to pray when things are going wrong and when they are going right. Do you mind if I pray for your situation, and for him?" Ty'arra asked.

"Ty'arra, I am not much on praying. That is why I am always taking care of myself."

"I know, Stephanie. You feel you are by yourself, but God is always with you. You have so much anger and hurt, Stephanie. You feel your parents let you down, you feel as if you let yourself down when that happened to you, and now the past is back to bite you. You must let go and let God help," Ty'arra said.

"Ty'arra, we can pray later," Stephanie said.

"That doesn't stop me from praying now."

"Okay, Ty'arra. You can pray."

Ty'arra placed her hand on her friend's shoulder and prayed in silence.

"Stephanie, let's go back out and enjoy our day. We are not going to let Satan take our joy."

The two went back out to the beach. Stephanie was a little hesitant, but after getting outside into the water she was okay. She didn't see Leonard again.

Chapter 7

"GOOD MORNING, JARRETT. WHAT'S ON YOUR MIND?" ANNA asked as her husband walked into the kitchen where she was making breakfast.

"Good morning, honey. You know, ever since I spoke with Mom, I have been feeling a little uneasy. I don't know what it is. You know we are close, and I can tell when something is wrong," Jarrett said.

"Why don't you call and talk to her?" his wife said.

"I don't want her to think I didn't believe her when I talked with her and asked if she was alright. She said she was. I am going to just call and check on her. See if she will tell me anything."

Jarrett pulled out his phone and quickly called his mom's number.

"Good morning, Mom," he greeted her as soon as he heard her voice.

"Good morning, Jarrett. Are you doing alright, son?"

"How is my daughter in law and my grand boys?"

"They are all good. Mom, you would tell me if something was wrong, wouldn't you?"

"I would if I couldn't handle it. Why are you asking?"

"I feel like something is wrong and you are not telling me," Jarrett replied.

"I am doing good, son. How is your job?"

"You know a lawyer's job is never done. The boys miss their grandmother. We haven't seen you since your birthday in February. Now it has been a couple of months."

"Your dad's birthday was just a few days ago. I went and put flowers on his grave and talked with him for a while. That was my best friend. My, how these months have passed!"

"We will be down in November. I wish we weren't so far apart."

"One of these days you all will get closer. Right now, you need the experience; you have just gotten your foot in the door. With all your hard work, you might become a partner there. I would like to see you all more, but your livelihood comes first. I am okay. I have been missing your father a lot lately, though."

"I know. I miss him too, Mom. Is that all that is going on, Mother?"

"Yes, why are you asking?"

"You seem a little withdrawn. Have you talk with Ty'arra lately?"

"Yes, she will be back at the dorm Sunday. She is enjoying herself. Okay, Jarrett, I have got to go, so tell Anna I said hello and kiss the boys for me."

"Okay, Mom. I love you."

"I love you too, sweetie."

How can I tell my son I owe the government $100,000? I can't believe it myself. If I don't do something soon, the IRS will take my Social Security and anything else I get. Why didn't I take care of this when I got money from Colonels' life insurance and my CDs? I wanted to go on two cruises and do other things. Well, I didn't know about the loan Colonel had taken out against the house then. I will make it. I am not completely broke. God will help me think of something.

Today is Friday, Caroline will be here today. I've missed her, even though I just saw her on Wednesday. Oh, the phone's ringing. Let me see if that is my niece.

"Hello, hello, Aunt Ophelia. I am running late. I had to run a few errands."

"That is okay, Caroline. Are you still coming?"

"Yes, I am on my way."

Since she is on her way, I will go ahead and make breakfast for the two of us. Hmm, this kitchen needs remodeling. I am so upset about the IRS trying to take my home. No time to think about that, we will have pancakes and eggs. Oh, that is Caroline now.

"Good morning, Aunt Ophelia," Caroline greeted her aunt.

"Good morning, Caroline. You look restful and nice."

"Thank you. I was going to make our breakfast."

"Go ahead and put your things away. I hate to be blunt, Caroline, but have you heard from your brother? He has been on my mind."

"That is why I am late, Auntie. Andrew told me he had a visitor at the office on Monday. He was busy, and by the time he went out to get the visitor, he was leaving. His receptionist told the visitor Andrew that it wouldn't be long, but he just got up and walked out. Andrew said from the back it looked like Patrick. He called out, but the visitor, whoever he was, never turned around. He just kept walking. I don't know what that could have been about. I was leaving home this morning when Andrew left and drove around the streets close to the company looking for him, but I didn't see him. I don't know his phone number or his address. I don't know how to get in touch with him. I love my brother; I just don't know how to reach him. I am worried about him, Aunt Ophelia. Andrew said he looks small, if that was Patrick at Andrew's office."

"Niece, please don't make yourself sick worrying about Patrick. Let's give him up to God."

"So much for that. What have you been doing since Wednesday?"

"I really haven't done anything; I worked in the backyard, planting flowers and just sitting out back reminiscing," Ophelia replied.

"You need some hobbies. I told you to volunteer at the hospital with Sarah."

"I told her I would think about it."

Caroline began her work and Ophelia started her personal tasks for the day.

"I am going to call my lawyer, Mr. Cannon," Ophelia said, picking up the phone to dial. "Hello, may I speak with Mr. Cannon if he is not busy? I want to know if it is okay for me to come in and see him today."

The receptionist responded with, "May I ask who is calling?"

"This is Ophelia Roberson. I am a client of his."

"Okay, hold on."

"Yes, Ms. Roberson. Mr. Cannon will see you, he is free for the next hour," the receptionist replied.

"I will be on my way," Ophelia said, then hung up the phone. "Caroline, I am going to run an errand. I should be back within an hour. If you must leave before I get back, I will see you tomorrow."

"Do you need me to go with you?" Caroline asked her aunt.

"No, I will be alright."

Ten minutes later, Ophelia stepped in the door of the lawyer's office and greeted the receptionist. "Good morning, I am Ms. Roberson."

"Good morning," the receptionist replied. "I will tell Mr. Cannon you are here," she added, picking up the phone. She spoke quietly for a moment, then hung up the phone. "You can go in, Ms. Roberson."

"Hello Ms. Roberson, I haven't seen you in a while," Mr. Cannon greeted his client. "Everything okay?"

"Hello, Mr. Cannon. Well, yes and no. I am okay, but I have a situation. I am getting letters from the IRS. And I didn't know Colonel had taken out a loan on the house. I don't know what this money is about. Do you know? I came to you because you weren't only our attorney, you and my husband were good friends. Colonel handled all the business. I don't want to lose my house," Ophelia's voice trailed off.

"How long have you been getting these letters?" Mr. Cannon asked.

"Well, I got my first letter in June," Ophelia responded.

"Colonel has been dead for two years, hasn't he?"

"Yes. Why am I now just getting letters?"

"Do you want me to call and see why it took so long and what your options are?"

"I would love for you to do that, if you don't mind."

"I don't mind. But that's not the only thing, why did he take out a loan on the house? "What was the money for?" the lawyer continued.

"I don't know. This is scaring me."

"I understand, Ms. Roberson. Let me check into this."

"Thank you, I appreciate your help."

"Have a good day, Ms. Roberson. I'll be in touch as soon as I've spoken to the IRS. Let me see what I can find out about the loan."

Ophelia nodded and stepped out of his office, closing the door behind her.

Chapter 8

"AUNT OPHELIA, ARE YOU ALRIGHT?" CAROLINE ASKED when she returned to the house.

"Caroline, I am alright. Just getting a situation handled. It is nothing for you to worry yourself over," her aunt replied.

"Okay. Yes, ma'am. Aunt Ophelia, have you been noticing anything about Tim next door?" Caroline continued.

"No, why?" Ophelia replied.

"I went out back to take trash out, and he was standing there. I thought he was coming over until he looked up and saw me. He is strange, he needs to get back in school. If I were you, I would keep an eye on him and make sure your doors are locked."

"I don't think he will try anything," Aunt Ophelia replied.

"Just be careful, Auntie, because I felt a little uneasy," Caroline insisted.

"Okay, I will."

"What do you want for dinner, Aunt Ophelia?"

"I don't know, dear."

"I am done with the cleaning, and I have time to fix you a small dinner," Caroline offered.

"Thanks, something light, please. I know you don't have time to eat with me."

"I'm sorry, Auntie. I am going to go home and eat with my husband," Caroline apologized.

"I know. Thank you for all your help. What are you all having?"

"We are eating leftovers from yesterday. We didn't eat very much, because we went out and did a little shopping. I bought this beautiful dress, Auntie. The company is having dinner next month, and I went to get a new dress," Caroline explained.

"With all those clothes you have?" Ophelia teased.

"I know. After that, we went to his parent's house. So, we were gone all day. I enjoyed our day out. We don't get too many dates. His mother fixed a big dinner for us because she said they don't see us very much, since Andrew is so busy."

"How are they doing?"

"They are doing great. With them both finally retired, they need hobbies, just like you do. His father plays golf and loves to fish, but his mother doesn't do anything but go to church like you. Maybe the two of you need to talk."

"I have one good friend that is married; I don't want all my friends to be married. Sarah's husband is out of town a lot. I want a widow like me for a friend," Ophelia replied.

"Why don't you start a widow's club? You would have a lot of friends," Sarah suggested.

"I know I would. I don't want a lot of friends, but that is something to think about."

"Okay, dinner is ready, and I am going to get home before it gets too late."

"Okay, niece, be careful."

"Remember to make sure your doors are locked," Caroline reminded her aunt.

"Okay, I will. And please remember to let me know if you hear from your brother. I would love to see him."

"I guess I will call my daughter and see how she is doing," Ophelia said to herself. "I don't want to bother her too much since she is taking a short break from school."

—

"Hi. Ty'arra. How is everything going?"

"Hi, Mom. Everything is going great. We are having a wonderful time. I think we all needed this short vacation without all the studying and reading. How is everything with you?"

"Everything is great. Caroline hasn't been gone for too long but I do enjoy her company."

"I know. Tell her I said 'hello.'"

"Jarrett said you all are going back to school Monday?" Ophelia asked.

"Yes, we are. I thought we had class Monday, but we didn't. I will probably be ready to go back to class by Tuesday."

"I am happy you are enjoying yourself."

"I am, Mom, but you know me. I would rather be doing my homework; I brought most of my homework with me."

"Take a break and enjoy life, baby."

"I am, Mom."

"There is no ugly stuff going on down there, is there?" Ophelia asked.

"No, Mom. We are doing okay."

"I can't wait to come home mom. It seems like I haven't seen you in a while."

"When you come, we will have our time to just enjoy one another. Bye, baby."

"Bye, Mom."

Chapter 9

OH YES, MY HUSBAND IS HOME.

"Good evening, honey."

"Good evening to you. Did you have a hard day?"

"Yes, I did," Andrew said. "You know, that is still on my mind about the visitor I had. I still think it was your brother."

"Did something else happen today?"

"I don't really know. I received a phone call today, but whoever it was would not say a word. My secretary put the call through, so I did not see the number the person was calling from. I asked her if the person said anything besides asking for me. She said no, he was silent in between her questions but he precisely asked for me. Not energetic or anything, I just said, 'Can I speak to Andrew Majors?' I asked her if she saw the phone number he was calling from, but she said she didn't pay any attention to the number."

"I pray he is alright. Maybe he will call back," Caroline said. "You know, I am still worried about Aunt Ophelia. She left today without telling me where she was going. She usually tells me. Something is wrong, but I don't know what. Maybe she will tell me one day, I don't know. Let's enjoy our evening together."

Caroline went home, and Ty'arra is having a good time at the beach. What am I going to do? Maybe I do need some hobbies or even to go work at the hospi-tal. No, working there would be too hard on me. I do need to do something to take my mind off this IRS business. I hope Mr. Cannon can find out something. Oh, the ringing never fails. There goes the phone.

"Hello."

"How is my dear mom doing on this wonderful day?"

"I am doing good, son, and how are you and the family doing?"

"We are good and blessed."

"I feel like I haven't seen you in a while, Mom. I can't wait for the holidays."

"I know, son."

"We took the children to Florida this weekend. We had a blast. I think the grown-ups enjoyed Walt Disney World more than the children. It was a quick getaway from work and everyday life. We are okay, just wanted to take an unplanned trip. How about you, young lady, are you taking care of yourself?" Jason asked.

"Yes, I am. I won't complain," Ophelia responded.

"I spoke with my little sister while I was away; I told her we were in Florida. She is enjoying herself. Do you know much about the guys she went with, or even the girl?" Jason asked.

"No, I don't. She is a pretty good judge of character, though. I don't think she would have gone with someone who is not trustworthy or if they are troublemakers. Why did you sense something wrong?" Ophelia asked.

"No, just wanted to know if you knew anything about them."

I asked about my grandchildren and then Jason assured me that he will be checking on me more often. I know that he senses something is up with me even though I tell him that all is well. The last thing I want to do is worry my children. We ended our call and as I walked away from the phone...

Oh no! As soon as I put the phone down, it rang again.

"Hello, hello? Sister Ophelia?"

"Yes, who is this?"

"I apologize. This is Sister Charlene Daniels from church."

"Okay. How are you doing this evening?" Ophelia asked.

"I am blessed."

"How can I help you?"

"The mission will be having a meeting tomorrow night at 7:00 p.m. at the church," Sister Charlene said. "Will you be able to come? I don't have all the details yet, but there is a family in church that needs financial help, so instead of us going to the church asking for money the mission is going to see what can be done to help. Their home burned down, and they had no insurance. They need all the help they can get."

"You can count on me," Ophelia said. "I will be there."

"Thank you. See you then," Sister Charlene said.

I am tired tonight, but I have got to talk to my Lord.

Before I talk with you about my situation, Father, I want to say thank you for everything and for everybody. Heavenly Father, I ask you to help the family that was burned out of their home. I thank you for letting them all be alright. God, I don't know what is going to happen with this situation I am in, but I know you are going to bring me through. I don't know what is going on. What did Colonel do? We were close, and I thought we talked about everything.

What was that noise? Ophelia was pulled from her prayer by a sudden noise. *I know no one is here. All the doors are locked ... there's the sound again. God, please don't let anyone be in my house. I am going downstairs, because it sounds like someone is in my house.*

Who's there?

I heard someone run out the back door. Oh my God, someone was in here. I am calling the police.

"911."

"Yes, I am Ophelia Roberson, living at 914 Aurora Drive. Someone was just in my house. Could you please send someone out quickly?"

"Ma'am, are you okay?"

"Yes, I think I ran them off when I came downstairs."

"The police are on their way," the 911 operator said.

"Thank you," Ophelia said.

"I am going to stay on the line with you until the police arrive."

"Thank you," Ophelia repeated.

"My God, how did someone get into my house?"

"Ms. Roberson, they will find a way."

"Someone is at the door," Ophelia said. "Let me make sure it is the police."

Ophelia turned on the porch light, revealing two uniformed police officers at the door.

"Ms. Roberson," one officer said.

"Yes," Ophelia replied.

"I am Sergeant Petrone and this is Officer Moore."

"One moment, I am getting off the phone with the dispatcher."

"Ms. Roberson," the dispatcher said, "I heard that the police arrived, so I will hang up. Please call us back if you need anything else."

Ophelia returned to the door and opened it. "Come on in, Sergeant, Officer."

"Tell me what happened Ms. or is it Mrs. Roberson?" Sergeant Petrone asked.

"Someone was in my house. And it's Ms. Roberson," Ophelia said. "I don't know if they took anything, or what they were looking for."

"Have you checked to see if anything is missing?" the sergeant asked. "And did you see the person?"

"No, I haven't checked to see if they took anything. I only heard someone run out the back door."

"Where is your purse?" Officer Moore asked.

"My purse is in my room. I always keep it there."

"We are going to check the outdoors around the house," Sergeant Petrone said. "We will check all the doors and windows. And we will take a report from you, Ms. Roberson, as soon as we check around the house. They probably had just gotten in the house when you scared them away."

"I am saying them, but it could have been one person," Ophelia said.

"Please keep your doors locked, and don't just trust anyone. You may be surprised who it was, sometimes it is someone you talk to or see every day," Sergeant Petrone said.

Ophelia thought about what Caroline had said today about Tim. *I don't think Tim would break into my house. Like the officer said, it might be someone I see every day.*

"Do you want us to take fingerprints?" Sergeant Petrone offered.

"Yes, but I touched the back door where he ran out, and I know I locked that door."

"Show me and I will check it for you," Officer Moore said.

Officer Moore checked the door and looked at the inside of the lock. "This is an old trick, Ms. Roberson. Someone planned this. Look at the lock; you didn't lock the door because there is clay or gum stuck in the lock. You don't know anyone who wants to hurt you or anything, do you?"

"No, I don't. This is scaring me now; someone came to my house and touched my door without me knowing. My niece was here today. When she took the trash out, she said my neighbor Tim was acting funny, like he was going to come over or he had been over already, because he knew my car was gone."

"We will go over and talk with him," Sergeant Petrone said.

"No, please don't do that. I don't want to get him suspicious or to start anything with me, just in case it wasn't him."

"Ms. Roberson, we wouldn't do that. We will ask if he saw anyone suspicious hanging around. Okay, Ms. Roberson?" the sergeant said.

"Yes, okay," Ophelia responded.

"We will be right back."

God, please help me with this. I don't know what is going on.

A few minutes later, the officers returned. "Ms. Roberson, we talked with Tim. He is really scared for you. We don't think he did it. He wants to come over. We told him that is okay, so he will come with you tomorrow. Let me go ahead and take your report."

"Okay," Ophelia said.

After all this, I can't go to sleep, it is too late to call any of the kids. I don't want to upset them. Everything is okay. What is going on, God? I don't bother anyone. Who was in my house? I don't feel comfortable or safe in my own home. Who came to my home and put something in my door?

It is so funny how quickly things can happen in your life. I was getting ready to lie down in my comfortable bed and now I don't even feel comfortable in my home. Ophelia began to pray, because she was a little afraid to go to sleep. She thought that person might come back, then figured he was long gone.

The next thing Ophelia knew, it was morning. *I guess God put me to sleep. And there is a knock at the door.* Ophelia was frightened, but she put on her robe and went down the stairs.

"Ophelia, are you alright?"

"Oh, Sarah. Yes, hold on."

"I saw the police over here last night. I didn't want to bother you so late, so I could hardly wait until this morning. Are you alright?"

"Yes. There was someone in my house last night."

"What?!! We don't have anyone breaking into our homes."

"We did last night. I heard a noise downstairs, and when I was coming down I called out, 'Is anyone there?' Whoever it was went out the back door. I was so scared."

"Why didn't you call us?"

"It was late, Sarah."

"Did they take anything?"

"Not that I know of," Ophelia replied. "I looked around, but if you are not looking for something or don't know what to look for, you won't notice it's missing until you need it."

"Have you called your children or Caroline?" Sarah asked.

"No, I didn't want to upset them last night, it was so late. I am going to call them today. You know, maybe I shouldn't say anything, because I don't want to accuse anyone of anything if I am wrong," Ophelia continued.

"What are you saying, Ophelia?" Sarah asked.

"Well, Caroline said she opened the back door yesterday to take the trash out, and Tim, our neighbor, was standing there like he was getting ready to come in."

"What? He is peculiar. He dropped out of school and is not working. I don't want to accuse him of anything, but let's be careful," Sarah said.

"You, too, Sarah, because John is out of town a lot," Ophelia agreed.

"We have an alarm," Sarah stated.

"Well, you never know. They might know how to trick those alarms."

"You are right," Sarah agreed. "And sometimes I sit in the house without my door being locked."

"I do too, Sarah. Now this has hit home. I don't feel comfortable in my house anymore. Someone I don't know was in my house. You know the shocking part? The officer discovered there was clay or gum in my lock at the back door. That is why it wasn't locked when I went to bed last night. I am so used to just turning the knob, I did not notice the lock did not go all the way through," Ophelia said.

"Yes, that is scary," Sarah agreed.

"I am going to get my locks changed today."

"And you need to get an alarm," Sarah insisted.

"Sarah, I am going to say this to you and please don't ask any questions about what I am going to say. I can't afford an alarm system. I am going through something right now. Please don't ask me about it, I have got to figure it out for myself."

"Ophelia, why haven't you come to us for help? Do your children know?" Sarah demanded.

"No, I don't want them to know right now. I don't know for sure what is going on. I have gone to see Mr. Cannon, my attorney. I can't get into any details right now, okay?"

"Okay, Ophelia, but I am not going to forget this or stop worrying about you," Sarah agreed reluctantly.

"Thanks. Please, just pray for me," Ophelia said.

"I am going to do that. Please call me, Ophelia, if you need to talk or need any other help."

"I will, thank you. I know you are a true friend."

Chapter 10

GOD, PLEASE BE WITH ME AS I TRY TO COMPREHEND WHAT happened to me last night. I am not feeling like myself. I know I have got to call my children, but I don't want them to worry even though I am shaken up right now. At this point, all I can think is that God will take care of me. I know he will.

"Hello, Aunt Ophelia. Are you alright?"

"Yes, Caroline. What's wrong?"

"Mrs. Sarah called me and told me what happened last night. I told you to watch out for Tim."

"Honey, we don't know for sure if it was Tim. I am alright, just a little shaken."

"I will be there in a few minutes, Auntie. I am going to have all the locks changed. Have you called your kids?"

"No," Ophelia said. "I don't want to call too early and upset them, I want to calm myself down first."

"Aunt Ophelia, I will be right over, bye."

I better call the kids before someone else calls them.

"Good morning, Jarrett."

"Good morning, Mom. What's up? Is everything okay?"

"Well, yes and no. I want to speak to all three of you at the same time."

"Mom, are you alright?"

"Yes. I am going to add Jason and Ty'arra on the line."

"Mom, you are scaring me," Jarrett said.

"Everything is okay. I just want to talk to the three of you at the same time. Okay, hold on."

"Good morning, Mom. What is going on?" Ty'arra asked.

"Okay, we are all on the phone, yes?"

"Hi, Mom," Jason said.

"Hi, Jason."

"My home was broken into last night."

All three kids shouted, "What? Are you okay?"

"Yes, I came downstairs and scared him off. I don't know who it was. They had put clay or gum or something in my lock so I could not lock the back door."

Jason said, "Are you telling us someone came to the house while you were there? Mom, that is scary."

"Mom, you need to have an alarm system put in the house," Jarrett said.

"Mom, I am coming home this weekend," Ty'arra said. "This is scaring me."

"It scared me as well, but I am okay Ty'arra."

"Mom, what if you had gone to bed and were asleep? He would have come upstairs. I hate to think about what could have happened," Ty'arra said.

"Don't think about it. That is why we pray to God and ask Him to protect us. Trust God. I knew he was here with me. I don't want you all to worry. I will be alright," Ophelia insisted.

Jason said, "Mom, we are going to worry. You are our mom, and we love you very much. We don't want anything to happen to you. Do you have an idea of who it was? Maybe you saw a resemblance to someone?"

"No, I don't. Caroline was here yesterday, and she said she was taking the trash out and she looked up and saw Tim either coming this way or he had already been here. She thought he looked suspicious."

Jason said, "He is the boy who dropped out of school, isn't he?"

"Yes, he is."

Jason said, "Mom, if you are not sure, don't accuse him."

"I am not. I want to make sure before I say anything. I forgot, the police did go over and talk with Tim. They asked if he saw anyone suspicious in the neighborhood. He told them no. They told him his neighbor's house had been broken into. He felt so bad; he did want to come over. They told him not to come over until today. Hold on, I need to get the door," Ophelia said.

"Who is it, Mom?" Jarrett asked.

"It is Caroline. She said she was coming over."

"Hello, hold on Caroline. I am on the phone with the kids."

"Okay, tell all of them I said hello. "Don't forget to tell them about Tim," Caroline said.

"I did mention it to them, but I am not sure if it was Tim. I want to be sure."

"Sons, I know you have got to go to work. I will keep you informed about everything," Ophelia said.

"Mom, it is Saturday," Jason said.

"I am sorry, I am just a little upset."

"Mom, do you need someone to come home?" Jarrett asked.

"No thanks, Jarrett. I will be alright."

Jarret said, "If you need us for anything, please call anytime."

"Okay, thanks. I love you all."

"Mom, are you sure you are alright? I can get my friends to bring me back sooner," Ty'arra urged.

"Yes, I am sure. Shaken up and a little uneasy, but okay. I am going to get off the phone and call the locksmith to get my locks changed," Ophelia responded.

"Okay. Mom, tell Caroline I said thanks for coming over and I appreciate all of her help."

"I will do that."

"Aunt Ophelia, do you want me to make you breakfast?" Caroline asked.

"I really don't want very much. Just make some coffee and I will have a Danish. Do you know a good locksmith who will change your locks and not charge an arm and a leg?"

"No. I can call Andrew to see if he knows anyone. I will get my phone and call him."

"Okay, thanks," Ophelia said.

Caroline quickly spoke to Andrew, then told her aunt that he recommends Jasper's Lock and Keys. "You want me to look them up?" she asked.

"No, I will look them up and give them a call," Ophelia replied. "I will be right back."

A few minutes later she returned to the kitchen. "I called them, and they will be out in about an hour. How long are you staying, Caroline?"

"I will stay as long as you need me, Aunt Ophelia."

"Thanks, sweetie, but I know you have things to do. You can go ahead and go home. I will be alright," Ophelia said.

"Auntie, please call me if you need to," Caroline repeated.

"Thanks. I will," Ophelia promised.

Chapter 11

I PRAY THAT MY AUNTIE WILL BE ALRIGHT. NOW, MY PHONE IS ringing. I don't like to talk on the phone when I am driving. I will this time because it is Ty'arra.

"Hey, cuz," Ty'arra greeted Caroline.

"You okay, Ty'arra?" Caroline asked.

"Yes, I am worried about Mom. Are you still there with her?"

"No, I just left. She called the locksmith. She is claiming to be okay, says she is just a little uneasy, like any one of us would be. You have a strong mother, though."

"I know. Are you and Andrew doing, okay?"

"Yes, we are fine," Caroline replied.

"You all are not talking about having children yet?"

"No, we just want to enjoy one another first. Even though we have been married for two years, we are still getting to know one another."

"I understand, that is a great thing to do. Sometimes you can live with someone and never know what they are like. Caroline, thank you for going over and checking on Mom. I will get off the phone now, because I have studying to do. Thank you so much for your help with Mom."

"You are welcome, Ty'arra. Take care."

While Ophelia waited for the locksmith, she realized that she had one more call to make.

"Hello Sister Daniels, this is Sister Ophelia."

"Hi, Sister Ophelia. Are you still coming to the meeting this evening?"

"That is why I am calling. I have had an unexpected disturbance at my house that I have to take care of."

"Is there anything I can do?" Sister Daniels asked.

"No, Sister Daniels, but thanks. Let me know tomorrow after church what was discussed, and I will see what I can do to help," Ophelia said.

"Thank you, Sister Ophelia."

"Sister Daniels, someone is at the door, so I will speak to you tomorrow after church."

Ophelia hurried to the door and opened it.

A tall, younger man stood there, wearing overalls." Are you Ms. Ophelia?" he asked.

"Yes, I am," she replied.

"I am Tony from Jasper's Lock and Key."

"Okay, come in. I want the locks changed on this door and the back door," Ophelia indicated.

"Okay, do you have the locks you want?"

"No, I didn't think about that. Do you all have locks?"

"Yes, but we will have to charge you extra for them," he replied.

"That is okay," Ophelia replied. "I just really want the locks changed quickly."

"Okay, I will get busy. May I ask you a personal question, Ms. Ophelia? Is it Ms. or Mrs.?"

"It is Ms. My husband is deceased. Ask whatever you need to, and I hope I can answer," Ophelia said.

"What is the situation that led you to change your locks?" Tony asked.

"I had a break-in last night," she replied.

"I am sorry, Ms. Ophelia. You know, these locks might not help. Did they take anything?"

"No. I guess I scared him off. He ran out the door."

"Ms. Ophelia, now another personal question. Do you have an alarm system?" Tony asked.

"I don't want to discuss that with you. I don't know you," Ophelia said.

"You are right, Ms. Ophelia. It's just that I know sometimes an alarm system will help. I don't know about your Christian life, Ms. Ophelia, but if you trust and believe in God, He is always there for you. He is better than any alarm system, locks, or anything else. An alarm system will scare the robbers off and at least alert the police, though," he added.

"Tony, I am a true believer in God."

"So am I," Tony replied.

"I enjoy talking about God," she added.

"So do I, Ms. Ophelia."

"Tony, I have gone through so much, and when I am in the presence of loving and godly people, I enjoy their company. I think God sent you here because I have been shaky all day."

"Thank you, ma'am. I am glad you are comfortable with me," Tony said.

"Can I fix you something to eat or get you a glass of water?" she asked.

"No, thank you. I am good, ma'am. But you can explain your curio cabinet to me when I am done, if you don't mind."

"I don't mind, I call it my Godly shrine. I enjoy talking about all of my ornaments inside."

"Ms. Ophelia, your home is cozy, warm, and comfortable. You feel like you are in a peaceful place."

"Thank you. I felt the same way until it was violated last night. I don't feel comfortable anymore," Ophelia confessed.

"May I say something to you? You said you trust in God. Don't let someone you don't know affect your spirit or the safety you feel in your home. As I put the locks on your doors, I prayed over them. I asked God to protect you from all hurt, harm, and danger. I don't know why your house was broken into; I don't know if it was someone you know. Someone could have been looking for something, I don't know. I don't know if they or he will be back, but I do know that God is with you, and he will never leave you. When you lay down tonight, give it to God and rest in peace," Tony advised.

"Thank you so much. You know, Tony, I am always telling others to trust in God and that everything will be all right. Now I have someone, a stranger, telling me everything is going to be alright."

"We are not strangers, ma'am, we are two people who God has put together. Now, I am done, and I have got to go. Here are your new keys."

"I know you are busy, so I will explain my shrine quickly. This is my biblical shrine. I started saving biblical articles when my late husband and I were stationed in Israel. I have collected them all these years. I feel they are a part of my husband and me."

"That is wonderful, Ms. Ophelia. I hope we meet again, but under different circumstances. Have a good day, Ms. Ophelia."

"You do the same, Tony," Ophelia said.

"I hate to rush off, but my father is in the hospital, and I am going to see him."

"I am sorry to hear that. Is he going to be okay?"

"I don't know. He is very secretive, but I trust in God," Tony replied.

"Take care of yourself, Ms. Ophelia."

"I will, thanks, and I will pray for your father."

"Thank you, that means a lot to me. See, we are not strangers. God bless," Tony added as he left.

Chapter 12

TY'ARRA LOOKED UP WHEN A KNOCK AT THE DOOR INTER-rupted her studying. It was Stephanie. Stephanie was not surprised that Ty'arra was reading as usual. Despite her friend's nerdiness, she finds solace in Ty'arra's company.

"Don't you get enough of reading?" Stephanie demanded.

"No. I enjoy reading. Now, I know you do not want to talk about me, so what's up?"

"Well, Ty'arra, we haven't had a chance to talk since we got back," Stephanie replied.

"I know. I haven't stopped praying for you and your family. I know you love your family, but I feel that sometimes there are situations that parents probably don't know how to handle. You go ahead and talk, Stephanie. I will listen."

"Thanks, Ty'arra. I hate that I saw Leonard. It just brought back old memories, things I have been trying to bury."

"I know. Hopefully, he won't try to bother you or anything."

"He doesn't know where I am," Stephanie replied.

"Stephanie, if he really wanted to find you, there are ways. People talk, and you don't know who knows who. Have you spoken with your parents to tell them what happened?"

"No, my parents are not very good listeners, everything is their way or no way. They would tell me to forget about what happened back then and say that there is nothing Leonard can do to them or me. I am their only daughter, and I feel like I am out in this world by myself. I have a brother who is older than me, but we are not close. I don't know why. My parents know I am not doing very well in school, but they continue to pay so I will not have to go back home. They don't want me home," Stephanie finished in a whisper.

"Stephanie, why aren't you doing well in school? All you have to do is worry about yourself and concentrate on your schooling. This is your life, your independence. When you get your degree, it will pay off in the future. I am not your mother, but I see a young girl with potential and I care about you as a friend and as a child of God," Ty'arra said.

"Okay, there you go with your God," Stephanie scoffed.

"Stephanie, that is how I make it, and by my mom's prayers. I don't want my mom's money to waste, or my time. I do what I must do to pass. I enjoy what I am going to school for. Your life is in your hands, don't just let it slip away and not accomplish anything. Grasp all the knowledge you can, and let it work for you. Are you going to continue your major in Fashion Design?"

"I love beautiful clothes and enjoy putting outfits together. I would love to become an advertising fashion designer or a television actress," Stephanie replied.

"Then keep your goal in front of you and don't allow your emotions to throw you off balance," Ty'arra said.

"Thank you so much, Ty'arra. You are a true friend," Stephanie said.

"You are welcome, Stephanie."

"I am going to leave so you can get back to your reading. I might go to my dorm and read, too," Stephanie said.

Stephanie dials her mom's phone number.

"Hello, Mom."

"Hi, Stephanie. How are you?"

"I am good. I was calling to let you know we are back, but the trip was a little awkward."

"Why? What happened?"

"Well, when I went to the beach to swim and have a good time with my friends, of all people, I saw Leonard."

"Oh no! What did he say or want?"

"He was ugly to me, Mom. He said he was at the hospital when I went that night."

"We didn't see him," her mom said immediately.

"No, we didn't see him," Stephanie repeated. "He is accusing us of killing his baby on purpose."

"Stephanie, he can't say that. He doesn't know what happened. Don't listen to him, he is just running his mouth. He really should have gone to jail, but we were trying to help his parents. Stephanie, when you come home, we need to talk," her mom said.

"What about Mom?"

"I will let you know when you come home. When will you be here?"

"I wasn't coming until the holidays, but if you need me to come home sooner, I will. Is Daddy okay?"

"Yes, he is. We just need to talk."

"Okay, Mama. I will let you know when I am coming," Stephanie said.

"Okay. Talk with you later."

"Okay, Mom."

Chapter 13

A SUDDEN KNOCK ON THE DOOR ALMOST STARTLED
Ty'arra.

Ty'arra lifted her head from her reading. "Who is it?"

"It's Craig."

"Hold on, Craig," she said, tucking a bookmark in her page and standing slowly.

"Hey what's up?" he greeted her as she opened the door.

"Nothing, I haven't seen you since we got back, everything okay?" she asked.

"Yes. What is going on with you?"

"Nothing's going on, just going to classes," she replied.

"Ty'arra, may I talk to you?" Craig asked.

"Sure," she said. "About what?"

"Did you enjoy yourself on the trip?" he asked cautiously.

"Yes, I did, but I didn't like it when we got pulled over," she replied.

"I apologize for that, Ty'arra. I am glad I threw the joint out of the car, so we didn't get caught with it. When we stopped at the store, I lit up a joint when you all went in, and I didn't see the cop parked across the street. He probably saw all of us black folks getting out of a nice car and could have seen me light that cigarette. He waited until we left and followed us to see what he could get on us. I am so sick of these cops attacking us. That is what I call it, 'attacking us.' I appreciate it when they do their job, but you wouldn't believe how many times I have gotten pulled over by the cops. I think it's because of this car. The only thing I do sometimes is smoke a little joint. Not all the time, though. He just knew he was going to find something. I thank God he didn't put something in the car. He knew he didn't have anything on us, so that is why he gave us a warning saying I didn't stop at that stop sign. I follow the highway signs and speed limits," Craig said.

"It is all over now. Let's put that behind us," Ty'arra replied.

"Yes, I don't want to get mad again. You want to go out tonight?" he asked.

"Go out where? Is anyone else going?"

"No, it will be just the two of us."

"Yes, why not. But you know I don't go out to those places you go to, Craig."

"What kind of places are you referring to? I do have a little class. Not as much as you do, but some," he replied.

Craig smiled. Ty'arra blushed.

"Yes, I am not categorizing you. I do need a break from these books. Stephanie was over earlier; you want me to ask her to go with us?"

"Well, I like Stephanie and everything, but tonight I want it to be just the two of us, if you don't mind."

"That is okay with me, Craig. Give me thirty minutes and I will be ready. How should I dress?"

"Dress casual," he replied. "And okay, I will be back in about thirty minutes."

Now my phone is ringing, and I am trying to hurry and get dressed, Ty'arra thought.

"Hello," she said, picking up the phone.

"Hello, Ty'arra."

"Hey, Stephanie. Anything wrong?"

"No, I just got off the phone with my mother."

"That is a good thing, right?"

"Yes, it was," Stephanie replied. "She actually had time to talk to me."

"That is great, Stephanie. I would love to hear what you all talked about, but Craig just left and wants to take me out to eat."

"Okay, I understand. Enjoy yourself."

"Thanks, I will. I will call you when I get back," Ty'arra replied.

"No, we can wait until tomorrow, because I want to know all of the details about your date," Stephanie promised.

"It is not a date; he just wants to get out" Ty'arra insisted.

"Okay, whatever you say. Have fun, girl."

Chapter 14

THIS IS A VERY NICE DAY TO GO OUT WITH A FRIEND. MY mother is doing okay after her ordeal. I thank God for that. My brothers and their families are okay. I will enjoy having male company for an evening. I deserve to go out every now and then, Ty'arra was giving herself a pep talk when there was a knock on the door.

"Almost ready, Craig," she called.

"I will wait for you in the car," he replied.

"Okay, thanks. I'll be down in a minute."

"I said dress casual. Ty'arra, you look beautiful," Craig said when she opened the door to his van.

"Thank you, but I am dressed casually. I don't get out very much."

"I know, you keep your head in those books."

"I do other things," she said, "but I guess I don't do enough."

"You do look lovely."

"Thank you, Craig. You look nice, too."

"You don't have to compliment me. Just accept a compliment, young lady."

"Okay, thanks. Where are we going?" she asked.

"Have you eaten?"

"Not really. I had a sandwich and chips earlier."

"Okay, I am taking you to a nice place, but inexpensive. You know all our money goes toward this college."

"I understand. We are going to enjoy ourselves. Everyone is out walking and enjoying this beautiful day," she said.

"Yes, I know," he agreed.

Craig and Ty'arra went out and enjoyed a nice evening together.

Craig took me home after dinner and he was a complete gentleman. He even walked me to my door and did not try any advances, he just wished me a good night. I went inside and called Stephanie and told her about the beautiful restaurant Craig took me to called Chantilly's. I told her how much of a gentleman Craig is and how impressed I am of his goals to become an alcohol and drug abuse counselor and he would also like to become an Athletic Director.

"I am happy you enjoyed yourself," Stephanie said with excitement.

"I really did. Let's talk again tomorrow," I told her.

=

"Hello, Sarah. We didn't know you were coming in today. You are usually early," a friend at the hospital greeted her.

"I know. A good friend of mine had a break-in last night, and I went to check on her this morning."

"Is she okay?"

"Yes, she scared them off. How is everything here today?" Sarah asked.

"It is quiet so far."

"How is my special patient, Mr. Robertson?"

"He is good, and he might be getting out soon according to his chart. A family member called today, checking on him."

"Really? Was it a female?"

"No, it was a male. He sounded young."

"That is nice. I hope everything goes okay for him when he is discharged. What is he telling you? Is he going home to be by himself?"

"I haven't gotten that far yet. I am going to see him now though, if you want to come with me."

"Good morning, Mr. Robertson," Sarah greeted her favorite patient when she entered his room.

"Good morning to you, Sarah"

"How are you feeling?"

"I am feeling wonderful: I received a call from my son. He is coming to see me," Mr. Roberson replied.

"Great! Is he coming today?" she asked.

"Yes, he is coming today. He had a job this morning, and after that he is coming by."

"I hope I am here when he gets here," Sarah said. "I am not going to be here long, because I want to check on a very close friend of mine."

"Okay, is she sick?"

"No, she had a break-in last night. But she is okay, she scared them off."

"Good," Mr. Roberson replied.

"I am going to let you get ready for your son and I am going to check on my other patients. Mr. Robertson, I am so happy for you. I will try to come back around to see you before I leave for the day."

"Okay, thank you, Sarah. Didn't I ask you to call me Robert?"

"I will remember that. Talk with you later," she replied.

"Nurse Cindy, did Mr. Robertson's son come to visit him while I was on rounds?" Sarah asked her colleague.

"Yes, he did. I think he is still there with him," she added.

Sarah didn't want the nurses to know that he had asked her to call him Robert.

Sarah went into his room. There was a nice-looking young man in his room.

"Hello, Sarah, you came back?"

"Yes, I told you I would if I got a chance."

"This is my son, Tony. Tony, this is Sarah, but you call her Mrs. Sarah."

"That is okay, he can call me Sarah," Sarah said with a laugh.

"No, he can't. You know my father was in the military," Tony said.

"Yes, I do," Sarah said.

"You have a very handsome son, Mr. Robertson."

"Thank you, Mrs. Sarah."

"Sarah is a volunteer here. She is a very wonderful volunteer. I wish we had more like her," said Mr. Robertson.

"I thank you, Mrs. Sarah, for helping my father while he is in the hospital and for giving him extra special attention."

"He is very easy to help," Sarah said. "I enjoy listening to his war stories."

"Yes," Tony agreed. "He has a lot."

"Do you live here, Tony?" Sarah asked.

"Yes, I have my own locksmith company."

"What a coincidence. Talking about a locksmith, I need to call my neighbor and see if she called the locksmith. My neighbor's house was broken into last night, and I am worried about her," Sarah said.

"I just changed a lady's locks because her house was broken into last night. She was a very nice lady," Tony said.

"If you don't mind telling me, what was her name?" Sarah asked.

"I can't recall the name, but it was on Lincoln Street," Tony replied.

"That is where I live. Was it Ms. Ophelia?" Sarah asked.

"Yes, that was her name. What a small world. As big as Miami is, and we meet at a hospital and know the same lady," Tony said.

"Thanks, Tony, for taking care of my friend. We are more like sisters. We have known each other for years. We used to go on trips together as couples," Sarah said. "I am sorry, Tony, I start running my mouth and can't stop. I am going to let you visit with your father."

"I don't mind, Mrs. Sarah. We are enjoying your company," Tony said.

"Thank you. I heard your father might be getting out tomorrow."

"Yes, I hope so. I want him to stay with me for a few days before he goes home," Tony said.

"That sounds like a good idea. What do you think, Mr. Robertson?" Sarah asked.

"I am thinking about it," Mr. Robertson replied.

"Robert, I am a little reluctant to ask this question, but is there any way I can contact one of you just to check on you and see how you are doing?" Sarah asked.

"I will be happy to give you my number, Mrs. Sarah," Tony said. "Thanks for your concern and caring, I appreciate it. This is my card, with my home, work, and personal cell numbers. Please feel free to call anytime. Thank you again for all your help while my father was here in the hospital."

"No problem," Sarah said. "He made it easy, being such a nice and gentle patient. If I don't see you, Mr. Robertson, before you are discharged, please take care of yourself and I will be calling Tony to check on him. I might also stop by, if that is okay."

"We would love it," Mr. Robertson said. "Thanks."

"Everyone have a good evening; I am on my way home. My husband is coming home tonight, and I want to be there when he arrives," Sarah said as she left.

"Good night, Mrs. Sarah. Enjoy your days off," Tony said.

"I will, thanks."

What a beautiful October afternoon, Sarah thought as she left the hospital. *It is warm but the breeze makes it feel wonderful out here. I am so ready for the winter.*

I am going to call Ophelia and see how she is doing.

"Hello, Ophelia. Are you okay?"

"Hi, Sarah. Yes, I am fine. Are you still at the hospital?"

"No, I am leaving, but just checking on you," Sarah explained.

"I am good. I got my locks changed."

"I know."

"I told you I was getting the locks changed."

"I know you told me, but guess what? I met the young man who changed your locks."

"How did you do that?"

"Well, I will tell you when we get together. No mystery, just coincidence. I would like to talk to you in person. I don't care very much for these cell phones when I want to tell someone something in person. I am on my way home now, since John will be home tonight."

"Great. I am happy for you," Ophelia said.

"I am happy, too. It seems like he has been gone forever. I will talk with you tomorrow or Monday. You probably have church all day tomorrow."

"Okay, Sarah. Thanks for being a great friend. I wouldn't have it any other way. Tell John I said hello."

"Okay, I will.

Chapter 15

I WILL CALL CAROLINE TO LET HER KNOW I AM ALL RIGHT, Ophelia decided.

"Hello, Aunt Ophelia. Are you alright?"

"Yes, I am fine. I have been wondering if you have heard anything from Patrick."

"No. Have you heard anything?" Caroline replied.

"No. Is something wrong?"

"No, I guess he has been on my mind a lot. Or I have just been missing Sylvia. I miss my sister so much. I don't talk about her very much, because it hurts too much."

"I know, Aunt Ophelia. With what you went through today and last night, you probably needed her to talk to," Caroline said.

"I do. I wish Patrick would come around. He knows we love him very much and want him to be a part of the family. Maybe we should try to find some of his friends and see if they know where he is," Ophelia suggested.

"I don't know any of his friends anymore, Aunt Ophelia," Caroline replied.

"It's like he just left his family, and we don't know why," Ophelia said.

"I know, Auntie. He just left the family on his own. I don't know what to think."

"If you or Andrew hears anything, please let me know," Ophelia said.

"I will, Aunt Ophelia. You got your locks changed?"

"Yes, I did. I am okay. And sweetie, sorry to have bothered you."

"Aunt Ophelia, you are not bothering me. I am going to check the jails again to see if they have Patrick. I will see what I can do to find him. He knows where we are, because no one has moved."

"Okay." Ophelia responds with melancholy.

———

I love this song, Ophelia thought.

"Oh, how I love the name Jesus, oh how I love the name Jesus, it is the sweetest name I know," Ophelia sang. *I love this song. I love you God and I trust you. I am going through, but I know you are going to bring me out. Why would someone want to break into my home? I don't bother anyone. Well, other people's homes get broken into, so why am I any different? There was a reason for whoever it was to come into my home uninvited, knowing I was here. This is a scary feeling. People are bold and don't care. I am a little afraid to go to bed tonight. I know the locks were changed, but that doesn't make a difference to burglars.*

Tonight, I am praying to God like I have never prayed before. I know he is with me. I need to sleep. As Ophelia prays, she listens for God to talk to her. *I know God knows what is going on in my life, I just must voice it to him. God, after all that I have gone through, I still thank you for all your love and your blessings. It could have been a tragedy, but you saw that I was taken care of even though my house had been invaded. Thank you, my dear God. Goodnight my heavenly father and goodnight my Colonel. I know I don't talk to you much, my sweet sister, Sylvia, but I miss you so much. Take care of Mom and Dad.*

What a beautiful Sunday morning. I slept very well. I thank God for a good night's rest.

As Ophelia began to get dressed for church, she began to reminisce about all the good times and memories her family had in the house. *After Colonel retired from the Army, this is where we placed our roots and we've been here ever since. I guess when things happen in your life, you think about just how blessed you are. My children are well and doing okay. I am well and I have a situation, but I know it can be fixed. I am hoping.*

On the way to church, Ophelia noticed for the very first time just how beautiful God's world is and what he is responsible for. The grass turns colors in the fall, the trees lose their color and leaves. *It is not fall yet, but I am thinking about what will happen. It is the beginning of October, and it feels wonderful outside. I am ready to go to church this morning.*

I see some people getting in their cars. I guess they are going to church too. Some are mowing their yards. Some are just outside, enjoying their beautiful Sunday morning sitting on the porch with their cup of coffee.

Thank God, I am here. Looks like a lot of people are at church this morning, judging by the cars.

"Good morning, Sister Ophelia."

"Good morning to you, Sister Rachael. Thank God, He let us see another Sunday."

"I know I thank him every day I wake up," Ophelia agreed.

The organ is playing as Ophelia goes into church, speaking to everyone. *What a joyful noise I love to hear. I missed Sunday school, so worship service is beginning. I take my usual seat, still speaking as I sit down, just ready to hear God's word in song or in prayer, but most of all the word. As the deacons begin to start service, I look up and see Sarah.*

"Girl, you didn't tell me you were coming. We could have come together."

"I didn't know either; it was decided at the last minute."

"Glad to have you," Ophelia said.

"Glad to be here. We have a crowd today. I see. Looks like the congregation has grown since I was here last," Sarah said.

"People join every Sunday. Sometimes they come back and sometimes they don't. I guess they get caught up in the moment. God is real, not just when there is music or a sermon going on. He is good all the time."

"I hear you."

"Are you going home?" Sarah asked when the service was over. She had spent much of her time there watching Ophelia and could see that Ophelia had enjoyed both the sermon and the choir.

"No, Sarah, I must attend a mission meeting. I was supposed to go last night, but I didn't feel comfortable going out when my house was just broken into. If you want to wait, we can get a bite to eat."

"No, I am going to go home. John is home. He wanted to come, but he is tired from his trip."

"I do understand. That is great, go home to your husband," Ophelia urged as she hurried to the mission meeting.

"Good morning to everyone," Sister Daniels said. "We are going to cover what was discussed at last night's meeting. Several of you couldn't be here but thank God you are here with us today."

"The situation is that we have a family in our congregation that was burned out of their home. They have three children, and the husband just started working," Sister Daniels continued. "They had no insurance. The children are in elementary school, and they are going to need school clothes and supplies. They have a twelve-year-old daughter and eight-year-old twin boys. They are seeking all resources to get as much help as they possibly can. They are not just sitting and waiting to see who will help, they are trying to help themselves."

"Have you taken up an offering for them, Sister Daniels?" Ophelia asked.

"No, we haven't," Sister Daniels replied. "The pastor wants the mission team to see what we can do for the family before going to the church."

"Okay, what did you all come up with?" Ophelia asked.

"I will ask everyone that had an input to tell you what was decided. I relinquish the floor for open discussion," Sister Daniels said.

"I am willing to let the family come in and pick out any clothing they will need," Sister Ruth offered.

"That is a great idea. Thanks, Sister Ruth," another member of the group called out.

"I am Sister Franklin," another member of the group offered. "You all know I grow vegetables and I can eat food. I am giving away food and giving a donation."

Another voice praised Sister Franklin.

"I am going to take the children and buy school supplies for the whole year. I don't have any small children because they are all grown up. I will probably get under clothes that they will need, as well," Sister William said.

"Thank you, Sister Williams."

"You all are doing a great job," Sister Daniels said. "God is so good."

"I can take one of the children on and get what they need. You know my situation, but I am willing to help anyone any way I can," Ophelia chimed in.

"I want to say to everyone, I thank God for such a wonderful group of women. We don't have to do anything, but I feel so honored to work with you all. My heart is over-flowed," Ophelia said to the group.

"We feel the same way you do, Sister Ophelia. Let us pray and get out of here to our families," Sister Daniels said.

"I will contact everyone with all of the information you will need," she continued "I thank everyone in advance. God bless."

It has gotten a little warmer, but it is still a beautiful day. Ophelia smiles as she drives home. She enjoys looking at what God does. Sometimes she wonders just what everyone does when they go home from church, since she goes home and sits by herself. *That is okay, I enjoy being home. Sarah and John are home. I guess Sarah cooked dinner. I am happy she came to church today.*

I am home. I enjoyed the church service and am glad I can help one of those children. And of course, the phone is ringing.

"Hello, Mom."

"Hi, Jason."

"I am calling to check on you."

"I am okay. Just walking into the house from church and I heard the phone ringing."

"I was thinking about you at church, and I told Suzette I was going to call when I got home to check on you," Jason said.

"Thanks. I am okay. I enjoyed church service today," Ophelia said. "How are you and the family?" she added.

"We are doing good, Mom. The kids said hello. They are really getting big. I will have teenagers on my hands soon."

"I know. I can't wait to see them," Ophelia said.

Tell Caroline hello when you see her."

"I spoke with Ty'arra last night. She said she will be down this weekend."

"I know. I told her she didn't have to come, because I am okay."

"Well, Mom, if she wants to come, let her, please," Jason begged.

"Okay, I will," Ophelia agreed.

Chapter 16

OPHELIA HURRIED TO ANSWER THE DOOR WHEN THE doorbell rang.

"Sarah! What are you doing here? Isn't John home?"

"Yes, he is home. You know you are welcome to join us anytime."

"Yes, I know," Ophelia said.

"You know I told you I wanted to talk to you about something?" Sarah asked.

"It's not what I talked to you about the other day, is it?" Ophelia asked.

"No, it is not. I don't want to talk to you about that until you are ready and willing to talk."

"I know, thanks. And I'll let you know when I'm ready."

"I met the young man that changed your locks."

"Yes, you told me. He was such a gentleman."

"Yes, he is. I met him briefly. You know his father is in the hospital."

"Yes, he told me he was going to see his father in the hospital. What's up?"

"Well, you know I am always looking out for you. Ever since I met Mr. Robertson at the hospital, that has been his father's name. He asked me to call him Robert, but I still call him Mr. Robertson. When I first met him, I just felt comfortable with him. I felt like I could tell him my whole life history and it would stay with him. He is a wonderful man. His son is the same. He was very polite. I know you are not looking for a companion, I am just looking at him as a good friend. Who knows what might happen?"

"Oh, Sarah, that is nice, but I have so much gone on right now."

"I am not asking you to marry him, only get to know him," Sarah insisted.

"You haven't told him about me, have you?"

"No, I haven't. I wanted to ask you first to see how you feel about the idea."

"I am not going to say no but give me a day or two."

"His son said he might be getting out of the hospital soon," Ophelia said.

"Yes, he probably gets out tomorrow," Sarah agreed.

"How are you going to contact him?" Ophelia asked.

"I have my ways. No, I asked him if it would be okay if I contacted him and checked on him when he leaves the hospital. His son said to feel free to do so. He is going to stay with his son for a few days until he gets his strength back," Sarah said.

"What is wrong with him?"

"I don't want to get into his health issue right now, but I will ask him if it is alright if I tell you if you decide to see him or call him. Is that okay?"

"That is okay with me. I appreciate your honesty and discretion. Thanks for coming to church today," Ophelia added.

"You are welcome. Let me get home to my husband. He will be home for a while, I hope."

"That is nice. "You enjoy the rest of your evening," Ophelia said.

"You have a good evening, too," Sarah said as she turned to leave.

I am going to check on Ty'arra, Ophelia decided.

"Hi, Mom. How are you doing today?"

"I am doing great. I had a wonderful day at church. Did you go to church?"

"Yes, I went with Craig. You know, Craig is one of the guys we went to the beach with."

"Yes, you two are becoming a pair, aren't you?" Ophelia asked.

"Alright, Mom. You are rushing things."

"I'm not, you enjoy yourself. You enjoyed church?"

"Yes, I enjoy church wherever I go, Mom."

"I do, too. Sarah showed up at church today."

"That was nice."

"Yes, I told her I am glad she came. How is everything going, school and personal life?"

"I like all of my classes. Just think, next year in the fall I will be graduating."

"I know, time passes by so fast. You will be a nurse. Are you going to pursue being a nurse practitioner?"

"I am really thinking about that, Mom. Glad you asked. I do want to get a job and maybe go to school part time or online. What do you think?"

"If you are asking my opinion, we will talk about that when you come home this weekend," Ophelia replied.

"Okay, Mom. I am ready to come and see you. This is going to be a great weekend. We can pamper ourselves or just sit around the house and talk. I want Caroline to come over so we can chat. I miss her too. You all still haven't heard from Patrick?"

"No. Andrew thinks he came to his job to see him; he had a client in his office, but by the time he was finished with his phone call, his secretary said the man left. She tried to stop him, but he continued walking. She described him, and Andrew saw him going down the hall. He thinks it was Patrick. We haven't heard anything else, though."

"I can't wait to see you, Mom. I am going to get off the phone and let you make your dinner. I will check with you later in the week."

Sitting there, Ophelia began to think. *Speaking of eating, I haven't eaten. What am I going to eat today? I think I am going to pamper myself. I am going to order Chinese food for Sunday dinner.*

After ordering her food, Ophelia began to think about what Sarah talked to her about. She hadn't seriously thought about meeting anyone. *I don't know if I am ready. It is okay to think about dating, but when it is brought to your attention and probably meeting someone it is a little scary. I am lonely sometimes, but I am mostly afraid of cheating Colonel, even though he is not here. Sarah knows my taste in men. I am sure she has put a lot of thought into asking me if I was interested in meeting this gentleman. She must think a lot about this person. I am going to pray on this and ask God to guide me.*

———

"Stephanie, you want to ride home with me this weekend?" Ty'arra asked. "You are only a few miles down the road from me."

"You are going home this weekend?"

"Yes, I am. I just want to see Mother since she had that little break in."

"I would love to go Ty'arra, but you know how my home life is. If we get into a heated argument, I want my transportation so I will be able to leave if it gets really bad."

"I have been told, Stephanie, that if you go somewhere expecting something to happen, it will. Go with an open mind. You said you and your mom had a good conversation over the phone."

"We did, but it might be different once I am in her presence."

"You will not know unless you try it. Always pray, Stephanie."

"I told you; I am not good at praying."

"You need to start. Talk to God like you are talking to someone that really cares about you," Ty'arra suggested.

"That will be you," Stephanie replied.

"Okay, talk to God the same way. He listens, and he will not leave you."

"Okay, that is enough about me. You went to church with Craig?"

"How do you know?"

"I saw the two of you."

"Yes, he asked me to attend church with him and that's all it was, okay."

"Okay, I got you," Stephanie said with a smile. "I will think about what you ask me, Ty'arra. I might ride with you; I don't know yet. But I will let you know before Wednesday."

"Thanks Stephanie. I will call later."

===

Oh, dear God, as I lay in my bed, I am thinking of everything that has happened to me within the past few days. Life used to be simple, I didn't have worries. Colonel was always there to handle all our situations. I have always trusted you God to take care of him and our family. Now I feel as if everything is on me. I am a strong woman, but I am not good at handling financial situations and dealing with someone breaking into my home. This has all thrown me for a loop. I still don't understand why it happened or what they were looking for. I guess these sorts of issues happen daily. So why should I be any different? Someone was bold enough to jam my door lock with gum. I have a feeling they were after something; I just cannot figure out what.

That reminds me I need to call Mr. Cannon tomorrow; I don't know why he hasn't got back with me. I know he is busy, but it has been a couple of weeks. I will give him one more week before I reach back out to him.

I guess I fell asleep fast because all I remember is talking to God. Now it is morning. Thank God for a good night's rest. I haven't had a good rest like that in the last few nights. Lying in bed I could hear the birds singing outside my window. What a beautiful sound! I wonder if they are thanking God for waking them this morning. They don't have to worry about anyone breaking into their home. But they do have to worry about protecting their loved ones from eagles and buzzards and other prey. Even with the ugliness in this world it is still worth living. Today Caroline will be here. I have missed her. Who could be calling me this early? What time is it? Oh goodness, it is 9:00 a.m., I overslept this morning.

"Good morning Ms. Ophelia," greeted Mr. Cannon.

"Yes, good morning Mr. Cannon. You must have heard me talking about you last night. I said I was going to call you today or give you a few more days," Ophelia expressed with a hint of anxiousness.

"My apologies Ms. Ophelia for not getting back to you sooner. I have run into a few issues, and it is more complicated than I thought it would be. Don't worry because I am going to get to the end of this. Don't call and speak with anyone from the IRS. I am going to handle this and get with you in about another week or so."

A concerned look covered Ophelia's face and she questioned Mr. Cannon to see if everything was alright but he would only give her general answers. Ophelia accepted the fact that Mr. Cannon needed more time, but she was trying her best to calm her nerves.

"If you get another letter, just call me and I will send someone to pick it up," Mr. Cannon said.

"You are frightening me a little."

"Don't be frightened, I will handle the situation. Take care of yourself, Ms. Ophelia," Mr. Cannon reassured her.

—

Ophelia starts a new day with positive thoughts. *This is going to be a good day. I claim it. Let me get dressed.*

As soon as Ophelia puts her clothes on the doorbell rings. *Oops, I forgot I had the locks changed and Caroline doesn't have a key.* Ophelia goes downstairs swiftly to open the door for her niece.

"Good morning, Aunt Ophelia. Are you ok?"

"Yes, I am fine, I haven't gotten dressed. I forgot I changed the locks, and you don't have a key. I am going to go out today and have a key made for you."

Ophelia noticed Caroline's figure and commented on her plumpness. Caroline knows her auntie is old school and does not bite her tongue on anything she notices.

Caroline blushed and then responded, "I know Auntie I might need to go to the gym. I tell you what auntie, let me see what I need to do here today and maybe the two of us can go out today together".

"I would love that, Caroline. I have only been in my room and the living area. I haven't done that much cooking."

Ophelia went to take a shower while Caroline started in Ophelia's room and her living area.

Caroline noticed something as she looked around to see what needs to be cleaned. *It doesn't look like I have much dusting to do. The house looks almost spotless. Maybe she cleaned to keep her mind off what happened. I hope the break-in isn't bothering her too much. I know it would bother me. She hasn't cleaned her gospel shrine cabinet. That is unusual. This is always clean and rear-ranged. I need to ask her about this.*

Caroline called up to her aunt, "Aunt Ophelia, have you had breakfast?"

"No, I haven't, I slept in a little late and had a phone call this morning. I just came down to answer the door when you came. I will be down in a second."

Ophelia came downstairs heading towards the door, "Caroline, I tell you what. You don't have to worry about cleaning today, let the two of us just get out ok."

"That is ok with me but are you sure?"

"Yes I am."

Caroline figured this would be the best time to ask her question, "I need to ask you something. You always keep your gospel shrine clean and spotless. I think it has the most dust in it and on it that I have ever seen. Why?"

Ophelia replied, nonchalantly, "I didn't notice that. I thought I cleaned it."

Caroline had a puzzled look on her face. *This is not like my Auntie. Something is wrong.*

Caroline decided not to push her auntie any further with questions. She got her purse and headed out the door with Ophelia. Caroline offered to drive but Ophelia insisted on being the chauffeur today. Caroline is still worried about her aunt.

"Are you doing ok today, Auntie?"

"Yes, I am great. Do I look like something is wrong?"

"No, I keep going back to your shrine and notice how dusty it is."

"Don't worry I am ok."

Sarah greeted Ophelia and Caroline as they were about to get into the car.

"You two are out early," said Sarah.

"Yes, we are going to run a few errands. What are you doing out this early?" Ophelia smirked at Sarah.

"John just left for work. I am just so glad he is home for a few days," cheered Sarah. "I am going to the hospital for a few hours. Have you thought about my offer yet?"

Ophelia smiled, "Yes, I will get back with you."

Ophelia and Caroline got in the car and drove off.

Curiosity tapped into Caroline's mind. "What is she talking about, ?"

"She wants me to volunteer at the hospital."

"That is a good idea Aunt Ophelia."

"I am thinking about it. Let us talk about something else. How is Andrew?"

Ophelia knows she keeps pestering Caroline and her husband to start a family and she promised herself she would not bring it up, but the question still escaped her lips. "I know I said I would never bring this up but, when are the two of you going to plan a family?"

"We are talking about that. We are going on our third year of marriage, so we are getting close to deciding."

"Oh, that is wonderful, I am so excited," Ophelia said, finally satisfied with her answer.

As Ophelia and Caroline were driving, they noticed two children who seemed to look like they were in elementary school. "Look at those small children, are they walking to school by themselves?" Ophelia wondered.

"I hope not Auntie, it is not dangerous," Caroline said concerned. "The oldest looks like he is probably 8 years old and the youngest is probably 5 years old. Stop and let's see if an adult is with them." Ophelia and Caroline waited and waited for the kids to keep walking by themselves. There was a knock on the window. It was a policeman.

Ophelia rolled her car window down, "Yes officer."

"Is there a reason you are just sitting here?" the office asked.

"Yes, there is. We are checking to see if an adult is going to walk with those young children. You should investigate that officer" Ophelia answered.

"Ok you all move along, and I will talk with the children," the officer stood back and waited until Ophelia and Caroline drove off.

"Thank you," Ophelia said as she drove off. "I should have told him to do his job and leave us alone."

"Well, he was probably making sure we were not hanging around to harm the children." Caroline said.

"I guess so. I guess since that happened to me, I am a little paranoid."

"I understand auntie. Any leads on who broke into your home yet?"

"No, I guess we will never know who broke into my house."

Caroline asked about Tim. Ophelia has not seen Tim in the last few days, but she still does not want to accuse anyone without having concrete evidence. Caroline does not want to suspect Tim either, but she still urges her aunt to be careful.

"Let's get a key made before I forget. I want to have several made for the children too." Ophelia said as she parked her car in front of the locksmith building. We are going inside Tony's shop *Jasper's Lock & Key*.

"Okay! I see you are calling him by his first name," Caroline teased.

Ophelia ignored Caroline's teasing. "We talked a lot when he came. He is a very nice young man. Guess what else? I don't know if I should bring this up because I haven't decided yet. You know my neighbor Sarah?"

"You know I know Sarah."

"Well, she met Tony at the hospital. Before he left, he told me he was going to see his father in the hospital. Just so happened his father was one of Sarah's patients she checked in on and chatted with frequently.

"What a coincidence!"

"Anyway, she wants me to meet his father. She said he is a very nice man. Oh Caroline, I don't know if I am ready."

"Listen to your heart and it will not lead you wrong. I feel like you are going to look for too many reasons not to."

"How old are you again? You think you know me with such wisdom you have."

"I do."

"I am lonely, but I don't want to confuse lonely with frightened. I enjoy my life."

"I am not saying you aren't Aunt Ophelia. You have been married most of your life and you get used to having that companion."

Caroline saw that the conversation was making Aunt Ophelia uncomfortable because she was contemplating dating again. Caroline put her hand on her auntie's right shoulder and told her she did not have to rush her decision. They dropped the conversation for now.

Caroline asked if she wanted company while she went into the locksmith shop, but Ophelia informed her that she would only be a couple minutes. Caroline stayed in the car and Ophelia urged her to keep the car doors locked while she was inside because the break-in kept her auntie paranoid. Caroline locked the car doors after Ophelia went inside.

I will turn the radio on while she is there. Caroline thought to herself to keep her mind entertained.

Ophelia walks into *Jasper's Lock & Key* store.

"Good morning, everyone," Ophelia greeted.

"Good morning, how can we help you?" someone behind the counter asked.

"I would like to get some keys made."

"Hello Ms. Ophelia," Tony chanted as he came out from the back office.

"Hello to you Tony. How are you doing?" Ophelia asked.

"I am great!" Tony's face started to frown. "You haven't had another break-in, have you?"

"No, I haven't, and I pray I don't have anymore."

"How many keys do you need?"

"I need four made."

"If you would have come a little sooner you would have met my father. I took him home. I didn't want him to do too much. He can be very hard headed. I want to mention that I met a friend of yours when I went to visit with my father."

"I know she told me. She loved meeting you and she enjoyed her conversations with your father."

Tony smiled, "She is a sweet lady."

Tony finished making all four sets of her keys and placed them in tiny envelopes for her.

"How much do I owe?"

"You know what Ms. Ophelia those keys are on me."

"No, Tony, I will pay you."

"I know you will, but I don't want you to. Have a blessed day and call me anytime if you need to."

"Thank you so very much Tony."

"You are welcome."

While Caroline is sitting in the car listening to the radio, she hears a song that she enjoys. Looking up from the radio Caroline sees a man walking with a jacket in 80-degree weather wandering around as if he were lost. *It is not cold for that man to be wearing a jacket. What is he hiding from or what is he doing? Hold on, that walk. That is Patrick.* Caroline jumps out of the car hollering at the man.

"Patrick!"

He never turns around. His feet began moving faster. She knew it was Patrick. *Why didn't he stop and look at who was calling him?* Aunt Ophelia comes to the car and sees Caroline outside glaring down at the street.

"What's wrong, Caroline?" Ophelia walked toward her.

"Aunt Ophelia I just saw Patrick."

"What, where? Did you call him?" Ophelia questioned.

"Yes, I did but he started walking fast and sped off. What is going on? What did we do to him to not want to see us or talk to us? I love my brother."

"I know you do, I love him too."

"He looks so small, Aunt Ophelia. This is the area where Andrew works. He has got to be living somewhere around here. If you don't mind, will you drive around, and we will see if we can spot him someplace? I could tell by that walk and the head. You know I haven't seen my brother in over a year. I haven't heard from him. Please drive slowly so I can look around." Caroline sits up and keeps her head on a swivel.

"What colors did he have on?" Ophelia asked.

"He has on a gray sweater and black pants or jeans. It is too warm to be wearing a big coat, but he had one on. You know how they are when they are on drugs, they wear coats and sweaters. I don't know what he is on. Maybe he doesn't have very many clothes and he is wearing all he has. Let's just look. I look, you drive Auntie."

After fifteen minutes of driving around aimlessly, Ophelia finally said, "Okay, we are not going to spend all day looking for Patrick because he still knows where you live, and he knows where I live."

"I know," Caroline said as she lowered her head.

"We will drive around for a few minutes."

"Thank you, auntie. It is like he disappears. I pray that he is not in any danger, Auntie."

"We will both pray for that. Let's go put some food in our stomachs."

"It will be my treat Auntie."

"I won't argue with you but next time it is on me ok."

"Okay, deal."

Ophelia mentioned that Andrew is always bragging about Mickey's where he goes for breakfast when he takes his clients out for brunch. They both decided to give Andrew's recommendation a try.

They arrive at Mickey's and get out of the car. As Ophelia and Caroline walk up to the front door, a lady just walks out of the restaurant wearing an eye-catching yellow dress.

"Look at that beautiful dress that lady is wearing, where would you get a nice dress like that?"

"Look at all these stores surrounding us," Ophelia looked around.

"Do you ever come downtown and look around Auntie?"

"No, I stay in my general area going to the mall."

"You need to venture out to other stores, Aunt Ophelia."

"No, I can wear what I have. I have got to watch what I am spending anyway." Ophelia quickly said.

"Are you okay, auntie?" asks Caroline.

"Yes, why are you asking?"

"You have been under stress even before the break in."

"I am okay, don't worry about me."

"You know I am here for you Auntie," Caroline reassured.

"I know. The situation will work itself out," Ophelia calmly blurted out before she could bite her tongue.

"So, you are having some problems or going through something. You know if I was having problems and Andrew and I couldn't work things out or didn't know what to do you know we would come to you, and I would want you to do the same, so why won't you confide in me?" Caroline pleaded.

"Caroline honey, listen, I am from the old school, if we can't fix our problems, we don't bring them to the children unless we really must. Let me tell you this about the situation I am faced with, neither you, nor Andrew can fix. Not even my children for that matter but, I am going to be alright. Don't worry. I am in good health, and I am not worrying about anything. Let's go eat." Ophelia brushed off the conversation and opened the door to the restaurant.

"By you saying that makes me worry." Caroline slowly followed behind Ophelia inside..

Ophelia and Caroline wait a few minutes until someone comes to seat them. A waiter came and asked about their party size. Ophelia put up two fingers but expressed that she would like a booth and the waiter showed them to a nice booth by the big windows.

"This must be women's day because look at all these women in here this morning."

"Yes, I know I guess they have gotten the kids off to school and the husband off to work and they are treating themselves to a comforting breakfast," Caroline said.

After they got seated and settled. The waiter asked, "May I get you all something to drink?"

"Aunt Ophelia orders what you want."

Ophelia looked at their list of drinks. "May I have an orange juice please?"

"Sure," the waiter responded.

Caroline gave her order, "I will have orange juice and coffee."

"Yes, bring me a coffee too," Ophelia said.

"Ok I will be right back," the waiter walked off swiftly.

"We are by a window auntie, maybe we will see Patrick pass by," Caroline hoped.

Ophelia looked upset, "I am not going to keep looking out the window hoping to see him because he has had plenty of opportunities to contact someone. You said he went to Andrew's office and left, you just saw him, and he took off. Let him come to you next time. He knows you love him and wants to see him. Let him make the next move."

"Ok Aunt Ophelia I will," Caroline changed the subject, "Do you know what you want?"

"Yes, I do, what are you ordering?"

Caroline got the waiter's attention to let her know they were ready to order.

Ophelia's mind ran on her son Jason. "Not changing the subject Caroline, but Jason hasn't called in a while."

"He called when you had the break in," Caroline reminded her.

"I know that was only a couple of weeks ago. I guess he is busy. I will probably call him when I get home."

"Aunt Ophelia, he is alright. Like you said he is probably just busy."

Aunt Ophelia and Caroline ate their breakfast and complimented the waitress on her great service and left her a nice tip. They got up and left the restaurant.

"That was a wonderful breakfast Caroline, thank you for treating me. I enjoyed our morning."

"I have too Auntie. I hope you are not ready to go home. I would like to go to this store before we go home."

"That is ok I don't have anything going on today." Ophelia stared deep into Caroline's face with amazement. "Caroline, I see so much of my sister in you. I sure miss her."

"I know you do."

Ophelia paused and concluded her thought out loud, "Maybe I should call my brother more often than I do. I haven't seen him since Colonel's funeral. He kind of reminds me of Patrick."

"He will not run from you, but he will stay away," Caroline said.

"We haven't had a disagreement or anything in the past. He is just a loner, I guess. If you need him, he is there for you though. When Sylvia found out she had the illness he was very hurt. He felt like it was our mother all over again. You know what?" Ophelia thought of something helpful. "Maybe Patrick has called him and spoken with him. When we get home, we will call my brother. I haven't called Joshua in a while. I guess I need to reach out sometime too and stop expecting everyone to reach out to me."

"Aunt Ophelia you do reach out to people," Caroline did not want her auntie blaming herself.

"I do reach out to church people but not my own family. With Joshua being in rehab I try not to bother him. I have an aunt in a nursing home, and I don't take time to visit her. Aunt Cecilia is my great aunt. I figure it may be because her mind is starting to forget us, so we seem to forget about her and that is not right."

"Well let's put that plan into action auntie and we will set time aside monthly to visit her. She does remember me a bit when I visit her. Turn here, auntie," said Caroline.

"Where are we going?" Ophelia interrupted.

"We are here at the mall," Caroline said as she turned into a parking spot.

"The mall? I don't want to go into the mall."

"There is something I want you to see."

"Ok, let's go."

"We are going to Macy's. You saw something today and you remember when Andrew and I went shopping a few weeks ago…"

"Yes, I remember," Ophelia said skeptically.

"I remember seeing something you saw today," Caroline said, trying to jog Ophelia's memory.

"Ok, what did I see today?" Ophelia asked cluelessly.

"If you don't remember you will see. We are going to the women's department."

Where did I see it? Caroline thought to herself. *Oh okay, now I remember. I hope one is still here.*

A lady who works there as a store clerk dressed in red and black came up to Caroline and Ophelia as they were walking through the clothing section as if it were a maze. "May I help you ladies with something?"

Caroline stopped and looked at her with relief. "Yes, I am looking for a particular dress I saw a couple of weeks ago."

"Do you remember what it looks like?" the store clerk asked.

"Yes, come with me and I will describe it to you." Caroline and the store clerk start walking faster than Ophelia and Caroline's voice gets lower as she is describing the dress she is in search of.

I hope she finds this "mysterious" dress soon because my feet are starting to hurt from all this walking. Ophelia thought as she slowed down because she had no intention of trying to keep up with those young folks in front of her.

"Oh, okay I remember the dress, it is probably on the clearance rack," the store clerk said.

"Wow, already?" Caroline said in amazement.

She nodded. "Yes, we are getting our fall clothes in."

Caroline informed the store clerk that her aunt saw a lady wearing the same dress earlier today and she thought it was a beautiful dress. Caroline asks what sizes she still has in stock hoping that she has the size that her aunt wears.

"My aunt says she wears size 18 but I doubt it," Caroline shook her head in disbelief.

"You are in luck," the store clerk declared with excitement.

"This is a 16," Caroline stated.

The store clerk explained, "These dresses run larger than their size. You might want her to try it on."

Caroline took the dress from the store clerk and ran back to Aunt Ophelia who was striding behind. "Look Aunt Ophelia!"

Ophelia's was filled with surprise. "That is the dress I saw this morning. It is so beautiful. Why are you teasing me by flaunting it in front of my face?" Ophelia paused. "Is that my size?"

"It is. I want you to try it on." Caroline urged.

Ophelia loved the dress too much to refrain from the temptation of trying it on. She took the dress from Caroline and went into one of the dressing rooms. A few minutes later, Ophelia walked out wearing the stunning ensemble to get her niece's feedback.

Caroline gasped. "Auntie you look beautiful in that dress."

Ophelia looked in the mirror and could not resist the beauty of the dress and how it looked on her, but she felt the need to snap back to reality, "I can't get this dress Caroline."

"I didn't ask you to get it, I am going to get it for you," Caroline said firmly.

"I can't let you do that," Ophelia objected.

"You are not, I am doing this on my own," Caroline insisted.

"Thank you so very much niece!" Tears ran down Ophelia's face.

Caroline gave her aunt a hug. "You have been like a mother to me, Aunt Ophelia. I cannot thank you enough for always being there. I love you."

Ophelia wiped her tears. "I love you too, Caroline."

"Auntie, I just saw Patrick walk out the entrance of the store."

"What?" Ophelia turned her head to see where Caroline was gazing.

"I know he is around Aunt Ophelia, but we will not be able to catch him. Why is he running from us?"

"I don't know, baby. Maybe he didn't know it was us."

"He knows this car from earlier when I called his name."

Caroline saw her aunt sobbing. "Aunt Ophelia, why are you crying again? Don't cry. I know how you feel."

"That is my nephew that I love as much as I love my sons and he feels as if he can't come to us not even me and I am supposed to watch over him."

Caroline put her hand on her auntie's shoulder to comfort her. "Aunt Ophelia, Patrick is a grown man. I am giving you the same advice you gave me. I know we know he is alright. He probably watched us the whole time. He has probably been watching us all day."

"I will get out of this dress so you can purchase it and then we can go home," Ophelia said as she walked back into the dressing room.

"Jason, if you don't get a move on you are going to be late for work this morning," Suzette said in an urgent tone.

"I am going honey, I just have a lot on my mind."

"I know you do, and I have noticed that. What's wrong, honey?"

"I don't have time to get into it right now, but I will be alright."

"Are you concerned about your mom?" Suzette asked.

"Yes, I really don't know why because I know mom is going to be alright. Something is bothering me, and I can't figure it out. Like I am supposed to know something or remember something, and I can't figure it out."

"You know what your mom would say…"

"I know, pray about it. You know, that is what I am going to do about these feelings, I am giving the whole situation to God. Thanks honey. I will call her when I get home tonight to see how she is doing."

"That is a good idea. Have a good day." Suzette hugged and kissed her husband.

Jason left the house, got in the car, and started driving to work but thoughts continued to race through his mind. *I think I will call my brother when I get to work if I have time. I don't know what is going on with me. Like I said earlier, I will give it to God. I do feel like I am supposed to know something or do something. It is really bothering me. Well, I am at work now so I will put these thoughts on pause.*

—————

"Good morning, Melanie," Jason greeted.

"Good morning Mr. Roberson," his secretary said cheerfully.

"If I don't have anything scheduled for the next hour, I am going to make a personal call and just take a message if anyone calls."

"Yes, sir I will."

As soon as Jason sets his briefcase down, he picks up the phone and dials his brother's phone number.

"Hello Jarrett. How is everything going brother?"

"It is all going well. What's up with you brother?"

"You know I have been thinking about mama a lot."

"I have too." Jarrett said in agreement.

"I was talking about her this morning with Suzette. You know Jarrett, I have been concerned about mom since the break in. I know she is a praying lady." Jason said convincingly.

"She is a praying lady but the last couple of times I spoke with her she didn't even mention God in any way," Jarrett informed. "Maybe she has a lot on her mind."

"I told Suzette I am going to call her when I get home after work. "Let me know if she shares anything with you which I doubt. I am glad Ty'arra is going home this weekend." Jarrett said.

"I know. I am happy she is going home."

"I know Caroline is there, but I just want one of us to go check on her."

"Jarrett, have you ever had something bother you and you can't remember what it is or what you are supposed to know?"

"No, is something wrong?" Jarrett asks with concern in his voice.

"I don't know but something is bothering me, and I don't know what it is about."

"I am going to tell you what mom would say. Ask God to reveal it to you and He will. Trust in God Jason."

"I will. Thanks brother, enjoy your day and tell my family I said hello."

"You do the same," Jarrett said.

=====

"Stephanie how does your class load look this semester?" Ty'arra asked.

"It is heavy this semester for me. I have class all day Tuesday and Wednesday and one class on Thursday."

"I thought maybe if you didn't have a heavy load this week we could leave early going home," Ty'arra offered.

"That is ok with me. I have class until 2:00 on Thursday but I don't have any on Friday."

"Let's plan to leave on Thursday. You can do all your packing on Wednesday night, and I will do everything else on Thursday before you get out of class. We can leave when you get ready. First, is this ok with you?" Ty'arra paused so her friend could digest everything she just said.

"Well, I guess so." Stephanie said hesitantly.

"What's wrong? Why are you hesitating? You are still going, aren't you?" Ty'arra asked.

"Yes, I am just a little nervous with my mom and dad and everything." Stephanie admitted.

Ty'arra consoled her friend. "We have already talked about that. You are going to be fine."

"I don't know about all that."

"I am ready to see my mom, Stephanie."

"I know you are. You know we are going to be on the road late."

"I know but God will take care of us. My car will be gassed up and ready to leave when you get out of class."

"Do you think the guys want to go with us?" Stephanie wondered.

Ty'arra gave it a thought then responded, "No, I just want the two of us to go. Maybe next time I will invite them if they want to go."

Ty'arra offered to run any last-minute errands for her friend while she is in class, but Stephanie confirmed to Ty'arra that she has everything she needs for the trip. Stephanie planned to pay half for the gas money that Ty'arra would need but Ty'arra refused because she invited Stephanie, and this is a treat to bring her so she can make amends with her parents.

"Call your parents and tell them around what time we will be getting there," Ty'arra reminded Stephanie.

"I will," Stephanie promised.

As soon as Ty'arra hung up the phone, there was a knock at her door.

"Who is it?" Ty'arra said loudly through the door.

"Ty'arra it is Craig."

Ty'arra opens the door. "Hey, what's up."

"Hello Ty'arra, I just came by to see you before you leave for the weekend. Are you sure you don't need me to go? I don't live far from you."

"Thanks Craig we will be alright, as long as God is with us."

"You can't do better than that. I will miss you," Craig smiled.

"I will miss you too Craig. We will talk when I get back. Right now, I just want to go check on my mother and see her in person to make sure she is alright. God only gives us one mother and you try to protect them any way you can." Ty'arra said.

Craig leaned in to kiss Ty'arra. "What was that kiss about?" Ty'arra blushed.

"I just want you to know I will miss you while you are gone."

"Okay. Let me know when you make it, I will be waiting for your call."

"Please be careful and stay alert." Craig warned.

"We will. Good night, Craig."

"Good night Ty'arra."

Craig walked out the door. Ty'arra locked the door behind him. Though she tried to nudge it off, her mind was still on the kiss and heart could not help but skip a beat.

"Good morning mom, we will be leaving as soon as Stephanie gets out of class," Ty'arra informed her mom on the phone.

"Ty'arra, are you sure you don't want to wait until Thanksgiving? That is a long drive, and you have finals coming up for the semester," Ophelia could not help but worry about her children to keep her mind off her own situation with the IRS.

"I know mom. I want to come home this weekend and we will be alright."

"Ok let me know when you get on the road. Who's coming with you?"

"My friend Stephanie is from our area, and she will be riding with me."

After the conversation with Ty'arra and Ophelia ended, Ophelia's phone rang just two seconds later. *Now, who is this calling?*

"Hello Sarah. What are you doing lady?"

"Nothing I just got off the phone with Ty'arra. She is coming today for the weekend."

"That is great. Is it ok if I come over for a few minutes?"

"Sure, Sarah I am not doing anything. Come on over."

Sarah was over by Ophelia's house in less than ten minutes. Ophelia figured there must be something on Sarah's mind because she needs to discuss whatever it is in person instead of over the phone.

"You have been busy this week Ophelia." Sarah said after they greeted each other at Ophelia's door.

"Caroline and I have been running a few errands. We just needed to get out of the house for a while. She and her husband might be thinking about adding to their family. They haven't totally decided yet. Her mother would be so proud of her. What really bothers me is Patrick. That is another reason we have been going out so much this week. While we were out on Monday Caroline was sitting in the car when I went inside and had keys made and she saw Patrick. We don't know why he is being so secretive and why he keeps running from us. She called out to him, and he walked away faster. We hadn't seen him in a while, but she was sure it was him. We have been going out in that area to see if we can find him or wherever he hangs out." Ophelia brought the attention to Sarah, "Ok so much for Patrick what is going on with you this morning my good friend?"

Sarah shrugged. "Nothing I just wanted to come over."

"Excuse my manners," Ophelia said forgivingly, "Would you like coffee or something to drink?

"I will have a cup of coffee."

"Is John still home?" Ophelia asked.

"Yes, you know he is an early bird. He might have to leave for a few days but that is okay. I am glad I volunteer at the hospital. You still haven't thought about what we talked about."

"I haven't had time. I mentioned it to Caroline, she thinks it is a wonderful idea."

"What about your problem you are having with the IRS?" Sarah asked.

Ophelia lowered her voice, "I have spoken with my attorney, and he said he will be getting back with me. He did say if I receive any more letters, or any phone calls let him know. He really put me on edge about this because he is not telling me a lot about what he is finding."

Sarah reassured her, "Let him handle it he will get back with you. How are your boys?"

"They are good. I am ready to see them and the kids. I love my daughters-in-law too."

"I spoke with Marlene this morning. She is excited about coming home. You know they are going to William's house for Thanksgiving. They will probably be here a couple of days early, if not we will see them Wednesday night before Christmas," Sarah said.

"It is great that your children live in the same state."

"I know Ophelia. I never thought they would all live in Augusta, Georgia, but they are happy there and they have good jobs. Maybe we can all get together while they are all here."

"That will be a big family reunion with all our children here," Ophelia added. "How is everything going at the hospital?"

"It is a hospital, there is always something to do. I still want you to meet Mr. Robertson." Sarah said.

"Let me get back with you on that. Have you spoken with him?"

"Yes, I keep in touch with him. He and his son are wonderful people. I have invited them both over for dinner, he will be getting back with me. I will let you know," Sarah said.

"I saw Tim this morning. He came over and spoke with me. He really feels bad about the fact that someone broke into my home," Ophelia said.

"You think he broke into your house?"

"I don't know Sarah and I don't want to think about it. I don't think he did, and I just hope it never happens again. Something like that affects your stability."

==

"You know you can come and spend the night with John and me if you want sometime, whenever you need company," Sarah consoled.

"Thank you. You are the best friend anyone can have. Really you are like family instead of a friend. Have you gone to see your aunt Cecilia lately?"

"No, I feel bad. I should go tomorrow and see how she is doing," Sarah paused then asked, "Ophelia you are doing okay, aren't you?"

"Yes, why are you asking?" Ophelia was surprised at the sudden question from her friend.

"You know I have my reason for asking. You are usually bringing God's name in whatever we are talking about."

"I do mention God when we are talking about situations."

"You haven't lately that is why I am asking if you are alright."

"Yes, I am fine. You just haven't heard me when I mention God."

"Okay Ophelia, I will leave it at that. I am going to leave so I can get a head start on all my errands today," Sarah said as she headed toward the door.

I better start cleaning this house Tyarra will be coming this weekend. I don't want her to think Caroline is not doing her job. I have kept Caroline busy this week helping me with my personal tasks.

=

Tony's father was so elated spending time with his son, "Tony I am so happy, and I feel great thank you for letting me go on the job with you today, I am so tired of being in the house all day every day. Not that I don't appreciate you letting me stay with you. It is hard for me to stay in one place for a long period of time."

"Dad, you have got to heal and get better. I have got to make one quick stop before we go home. Since we are in this area, I thought maybe I would give Ms. Ophelia a call and check on her to see if she has had any more problems with break ins."

"Ok son," Dad stopped to think, "I have heard that name before."

"You don't mind, do you dad?"

"No son, go ahead."

Tony calls Aunt Ophelia. She did not recognize his voice at first until he mentioned that he changed her locks. Tony told her he was in her neighborhood and asked if she would like him to come by and check on the safety of her home. Ophelia mentioned that everything was going fine but since she is still a bit paranoid, she did not mind having Tony come to double check.

"Okay see you in a few minutes," Tony said. "Ms. Ophelia, I have my father with me. Is that okay?"

108

"That is fine," Ophelia said. *Before I could finish straightening up there was a knock.* "Hello Tony, wow, you were not kidding when you said you were right in the neighborhood."

"Hello Ms. Ophelia. My father can stay in the truck until I am finished."

"Do you treat all your customers so wonderfully?" Ophelia asked.

"I try to Ms. Ophelia. I want to make sure you are well pleased. Since I was in the area, I thought about you."

"Thank you, my children would be grateful to know a young man like you are checking on their mother." Ophelia complimented.

"I loved my mother dearly, but she is with God now."

"Yes, I remember you told me." Ophelia empathized.

Ophelia gave Tony permission to allow his father to come inside her home because it was impolite for him to wait in his truck.

"Ms. Ophelia, this is my dad, Robert."

"It is nice to meet you, Robert," Ophelia motioned Robert to take a seat on the couch in the living area."

"Thank you, you have a nice home."

"Thank you. My friend Sarah speaks very highly of you." Ophelia said.

I am so sorry someone came into your home."

"Yes, that was a scary feeling. Thank God you are okay. You never feel comfortable anymore because the person or persons that break in if they are not caught keep thinking they are coming back." Ophelia confessed.

"I know. We are going to trust in God and hopefully they will not come back."

"Okay, dad I am done we are ready to go."

"You all are welcome to stay for coffee or dinner."

"Thanks Ms. Ophelia I better get dad home so he can rest. I have had him out all day."

"Okay, thanks for coming by and checking on me."

Ophelia walked out with the men to see them off. As she begins to walk back into the house, she sees Tim walking down the street.

"Hello Tim." Ophelia greeted.

"Hello Ms. Ophelia. Have you had any more trouble, Ms. Ophelia?" Tim asked.

"No, I haven't Tim thanks for asking." *He barely looked at me. I don't want to think Tim came into my house, but he sure has been acting strange since the break-in. The police did go over and talk to him. I am not going to think he had anything to do with it. All these years we have been in this neighborhood I have never gone over to his house to be social toward his parents, not because I haven't wanted to but because they are not very welcoming. Anyway, let me go in and start preparing for Ty'arra's arrival. I have got to clean the house myself this week. Caroline and I did other things this week and I enjoyed it. I don't want Ty'arra to think anything negative when she gets here.*

My phone is ringing. "Hello."

"Hello mom," Ty'arra said with disappointment in her voice.

"Ty'arra are you alright?"

"No, I am upset. My friend Stephanie is not going to be able to ride home with me. Her mother called and asked if she could wait until Thanksgiving to come home. I will be driving home by myself."

Ophelia understood her concern and she did not want her daughter driving that distance alone. "Ty'arra I would feel more comfortable if you would wait also. It is only a few weeks away. I am fine and I haven't had any problems. I am well taken care of. Are you okay sweetheart?"

"Yes, mom I am just a little disappointed."

"I understand."

"Mom I will get on the road tomorrow as planned and come home if you need me to."

"No, you stay there, maybe Stephanie needs you there."

"I am going to get with her later she did sound upset," Ty'arra said.

"Ty'arra I love you and I am fine," Ophelia reassured her daughter because she know her children had been worried about her since the break-in.

"Okay mom, I will check with you later. I am sorry mom."

"No, don't be, things happen for a reason. Go ahead and check on your friend."

After they both said, 'I love you,' Ty'arra hung up and thought about Stephanie. Though Ty'arra really wanted to see her mom, she realized that maybe God has a reason why she needs to be here for her friend instead. She called Stephanie to ask if she wanted to come over.

"I would like to, but I know you wanted to go home, and I had to spoil it at the last minute."

"It was not the last minute we had a few more hours before we had planned to leave. I am okay Stephanie don't beat yourself up." Ty'arra said. "Plus, my mom is okay and that is what matters, so come over and we can have hot chocolate and cookies."

Stephanie cheered up, "I will be there shortly Ty'arra."

While Ty'arra was waiting for Stephanie to come she went ahead and unpacked her bags and put her clothes away. Stephanie arrived at her door fifteen minutes later. They enjoyed their evening together and it was uplifting for them both, and it helped get their minds off the disruption in their plans to drive home.

Ty'arra voice changed to a serious tone, "Stephanie I am concerned about you. Are your parents, okay?"

"I don't know. My mother called me after I got out of class, and she didn't sound the way she did the last time I spoke with her. She was distant. I am familiar with her when she is like that because that is how she was before I came to school. This time it was different. I hope they are alright. I asked her if dad was home, and she said not yet. She did tell me that she loves me. I don't hear that very often.

Ty'arra encouraged her friend, "If something is wrong let them work it out. You know I always tell you to pray about the situations as they arise."

"I know and I am getting there," Stephanie said softly.

At the end of their conversation, Ty'arra thought it would be a great idea to watch a movie. Ty'arra asked Stephanie if she wanted to go, and she agreed.

An evening to eat buttery popcorn and gain a few pounds is just what two young ladies who are concerned about their parents need.

Ty'arra called Craig to let him know that she was not going to be driving to her mom's house but instead going to the movies with her friend Stephanie. Craig was happy to know that Ty'arra was still going to be in town, but he knew that she was still concerned about her mom, so he was glad she is going out to put her mind at ease.

"I think it's something going on with you and Craig," Stephanie teased.

"We are just good friends Stephanie," Ty'arra tried to convince Stephanie, but she was having a hard time believing that they were "just" friends herself.

═══

"Who was that asking about me on the phone?" Frank asked.

"That was Stephanie," Mary replied.

"Is Stephanie alright? Is she still coming with her friend Ty'arra?"

"I asked her to wait until Thanksgiving,"

Frank got upset. "That is the problem you are always making the decision for both of us and not consulting me about anything."

"We are going through a lot Frank, and I didn't want her to come home and be in the middle."

"Mary, I am really hurt behind you and your decision making. We have been married all these years and I feel like I don't know you."

"We have both been interested in just what we are doing and no one else. I get involved in my job and you get involved in your job and whatever else you do; I can confidently say I don't know you either."

"When Leonard came to my office and said he was the father of my grandchild that you and Stephanie got rid of. He said he was going to get even because you and Stephanie got rid of his child. I told him to leave my office.

I wanted to kill him after he did what he did to Stephanie. That was rape and we didn't protect her then and we are still not protecting her. I am glad she has this friend Ty'arra because we sure as hell haven't been there for her. I never wanted to see Leonard again after that night. I never knew about any pregnancy. I never knew any of this Mary. You told me Stephanie was on her cycle after that happened to her and she was having bad stomach problems. That is when you took her to the hospital!" Frank's voice was getting louder.

"Frank, you should sit down so we can talk," Mary said calmly, trying to calm down her husband.

"Mary, we needed to talk years ago. I am living in a house with a stranger. You should have let me talk to my daughter. She probably thinks I don't love her. I know she was doing things. It wasn't her fault we never took time with her. We just thought if we gave her everything she wanted she would be ok. We forgot to give her the most important thing and that was us. She did not hear the words 'I love you' enough from us. You are her mother, you should have been more sympathetic with her."

"Don't just put it on me! You live here too, and you are her father," Mary objected.

"I am going to call Stephanie and tell her I knew nothing about her pregnancy. She stayed in her room all the time when she wasn't out with her friends. I am glad it was summertime," said Frank.

—

"Mary, you know that grandchild belonged to both of us. I know *how* it happened was wrong, but we had an obligation to our daughter, and you took mine from me." Frank said.

"We took all our obligations from each other because we were too busy worrying about what people might think and what they will say. We never considered our daughter and what she went through," Mary said.

"Frank, I told my daughter I love her a few days ago and I have never told her that. Can you imagine how that must feel to her? I know my mother never told me she loves me, so I know how Stephanie feels. I should have learned from that. We have been wrong in so many ways. That man that raped our daughter should be behind bars. I asked Stephanie not to come home this weekend because we need to work on us and what we did as parents. Either you agree with me or not and if you are so hurt and disappointed in me that you can't stay, I understand," Mary lowered her face.

"I love you, Mary. We never really told one another that we love each other. I am telling you now."

"I love you and I hope you will stay. We need to start seeking help."

"If you don't mind, I would like to speak with my daughter. Now that we have started talking, I would like to tell my daughter I love her." Frank said.

"That is a start. We can talk later. I guess that is why we don't have a relationship with Charles and his family either. I love our son. We should try to contact him after we talk." Mary suggested.

Before Frank called his daughter he began to think about his life as a small boy. *My dad used to take me to work with him. I noticed my dad doing and saying things that I knew weren't right or the truth. My dad had a log cabin business with a friend of his name Thomas, but everyone called him Colonel. Something went wrong in the business, but I never understood what. The same thing happened between my son and me. I guess I didn't have time for him either. Now he has his own family, and he doesn't take time to call us. Mary and I do need to call Charles as well. We have got to get our family back together. I hope it is not too late for us and our children to have a loving relationship. I do love them very much.*

"I am going to go upstairs and call Stephanie, we need to talk," Frank said. "Mary, did she say she was going anywhere?"

"No, she is probably upset because I called her at the last minute and asked her not to come this weekend," Mary admitted.

Frank dialed Stephanie's number, but the phone kept ringing and then went to voicemail. "She didn't answer. I will call her back later."

"We still need to talk to Frank because there is something I have not told you. Do you remember when Stephanie went to the beach with some of her classmates?"

"Yes, I remember."

"She ran into Leonard at the beach of all places."

Frank sighed "Why didn't you tell me Mary?"

"I don't know, I guess I would've had to tell the whole truth and I wasn't prepared to do that at the time."

"Did he hurt her?" Frank asked angrily.

"No," Mary said calmly. "He accused her and me of killing his baby."

"How did he know she was pregnant?"

Mary took a deep breath and explained, "The night I had to take Stephanie to the hospital because she was threatening a miscarriage, Leonard was there with a friend of his that had gotten really sick at his place."

Frank's face softened, "How did Stephanie handle the situation?"

"I will say this even though we haven't been very good parents, we have a very strong-minded daughter. She has a very spiritual friend that helps her a lot. She said he did not frighten her with his accusations because she knew the truth. She asks him to leave her alone or she would call the police and tell them he is harassing her," Mary said.

Frank threw up his hands, "This is too much. We need to have a weekend of no interruptions. I was going to go to work for a few hours on Saturday, but we need the whole weekend to talk and get reacquainted."

"Yes, we do," Mary agreed with her husband. "You can go ahead and call Stephanie back while I take my shower and then we will sit down and talk afterwards."

Frank tried calling Stephanie twice but got no answer. "Well, she didn't answer. I hope she is alright," Frank sighed. "I guess she turned her phone off after talking with her mother."

===

"Sarah, I am going to say goodnight. Thank you for checking on me. I am going to call Ty'arra before going to bed. We will talk tomorrow."

"Alright Ophelia, have a good night."

"You as well, Ophelia."

Ophelia takes some of her clean towels and heads toward her bathroom.

"Well, I didn't get Ty'arra maybe she is out because it is still early evening. I am going to take my bath and relax," she says to herself.

"I will just talk with my Heavenly Father before retiring to bed."